'I'll pop the kettle on,' I say. 'By the time it's boiled I'll have the problem sorted out.'

'Mrs Butler look[illegible] and delivers herself of [illegible]ays.

'Have trust in [illegible] you down.' . . .

'But the room's [illegible] he window! You've b[illegible]

'That wasn't me, [illegible] be very dangerous if t[illegible]. Maybe I could fit –'

'No!' Mrs Butler almost shrieks the word, 'I think you've done enough for one day . . . Why don't you go upstairs and wash your hands? I'll tidy up down here.'

'I couldn't let you do that,' I say. 'That's *my* job. Once I get stuck into something, I'm a little demon.'

'Ye-es.' Mrs Butler looks at me with renewed interest and sucks in her breath. 'There must be something you're good at . . .'

Also by Timothy Lea

CONFESSIONS FROM THE POP SCENE
CONFESSIONS FROM A HEALTH FARM
CONFESSIONS FROM THE SHOP FLOOR
CONFESSIONS OF A LONG DISTANCE LORRY DRIVER

Timothy Lea

Confessions of a Plumber's Mate

Futura Publications Limited

A Futura Book

First published in Great Britain in 1975
by Futura Publications Limited

ISBN 0 8600 7198 7
Printed in Great Britain by
Hazell Watson & Viney Ltd
Aylesbury, Bucks

Futura Publications Limited
49 Poland Street
London W1A 2LG

CONTENTS

Chapter Six

In which Timmy gets to grips with Mrs Butler's plumbing and manifests symptoms of a strange and terrifying complaint.

Chapter Seven

In which Timmy seeks medical advice and takes off in the company of Doctor Grimdyke and an attractive sexual surrogate called Judy.

Chapter Eight

In which Felicity and Nancy work their therapeutic magic at the Indoor Outdoor Exhibition and something very climactic happens.

CHAPTER ONE

In which Timmy returns to the bosom of his family from the frozen north and attends an eventful dinner party thrown by brother-in-law Sid, and sister Rosie, for Mum and Dad. Also in which he shares an unexpected pleasure with another guest – comely Imogen Fletcher.

Forty-eight hours I am stuck inside Enid, give or take a few – and by the end of the experience I would rather give than take, I don't mind telling you. Of course, I am referring to Enid, my lorry, and the length of time I spend in a snow drift on the Pennines, not to anything more unwholesome. Not that there is a lot more unwholesome than spending forty-eight hours on a load of uncured sheepskins. Of course, I do have Shirl – I have to laugh when I write that – have her? We practically write a new sex manual together. What a woman! Once she gets to like you she is no slouch in finding ways of demonstrating the fact. One thing about those sheepskins, they are warm – I mean, the sheep wouldn't wear them if they weren't, would they? – and snuggled up together in the middle of them it is easy for the natural curtain of modesty that separates two young people to be drawn aside to reveal the elementary life force that surges like a mighty torrent beyond the cottage window. Sorry about that but when you're stuck in a snowdrift with a randy bird, a Worcester Pearmain and a bar of fruit and nut, your mind does tend to go off into the poetical. I mean, as an experience it can have its longueurs. Don't get me wrong. As regular readers will know, I am not averse to a spot of in and out. The trouble is that after forty-eight hours I am all-in and ready for the out.

It would have been even worse if the bloke from the sports car had not joined us. At first I think it is one of the Long Horns that has been sheltering against the back of the lorry – as it turns out, I am not so far wrong. I don't want to go into details because I find it too humiliating but he and Shirl strike up an instant understanding. I don't mind too much because I am able to get stuck into his barley sugar. Without that, I think I might be in a worse way than I am. By the time they get us out I am noshing the castor sugar at the bottom of the tin.

No doubt you recall the build-up to these incidents? I describe it in an account of my experiences as a lorry driver entitled, perhaps not altogether surprisingly, *Confessions of a Long Distance Lorry Driver*, published by Futura and available from high class bookshops everywhere. Readers of that tome will recall that Lady Luck has not risked a hernia through bearing me large slices of good fortune of late. The load of glasses I was carrying north went west and there is a strong likelihood of extreme unpleasantness with brother-in-law and partner, Sidney Noggett, when I eventually limp back to the Smoke.

When the snow plough gets to us, Shirl decides to travel with the bloke in the sports car. Simon Masterton is what I think his name is. He plays no further part in the story but I thought you might like to say goodbye to him. Shirl clearly reckons that they have something very big going for them and I think I have already alluded to what that might be. As far as I am concerned, Shirl turns off faster than the time switch on a Scotsman's central heating system and once again I am shocked by the changeability of women. They are like the weather. You never know what they are going to do next. I thought I was the best thing that had ever happened to her until Simon Jumbo-Parts shoved his long conk over the tailboard.

I have more bother when I get to Hull where I am supposed to be delivering the skins. At first they refuse to take them. I am not a little narked because I have spent a lot of time fluffing them out. It is a bit insulting, isn't it? I mean, they are not supposed to be cured and they niffed more than a bit when I took charge of them. Maybe I ought to change the Cologne I use. It makes a mockery of one's programme of personal freshness. Frankly, I can't see what the bloke is getting so worked up about. The sheep have it away in them, don't they? I would like to point this out but I can't give too much away about those two torrid – and rather horrid – nights without weakening my position.

In the end I threaten to shove them through the office letterbox one by one and the bloke throws in the sponge. Once I have used it to his satisfaction, he agrees to accept the skins.

As I drive back to London, a fresh worry invades my already over-occupied mind: the effect that my unexpected absence will have had on Mum and Dad. We say a few harsh words to each other but basically we are very close. I expect that Mum will be nearly distraught with worry and that Dad will be having to struggle to keep a grip on his emotions. I had better postpone my showdown with Sid and get straight round to 17 Scraggs Lane, the ancestral home of the Leas in the burrow of Clapham – that's what we call our street now because of all the high-rise flats around it. You feel as it you are underground. I park the lorry beyond the line of abandoned cars that starts outside our front door – actually, a lot of them aren't abandoned. Sid has borrowed them to come and see us and nobody has found them yet. Sid does have the Rover but it is always in the garage having the dents taken out of it – I keep telling him that he shouldn't drive at the traffic wardens like that.

I hope that Mum does not burst into tears or anything. Of course, it would be quite understandable if she did. Her only son snatched back from the living hell of the north; the new ice age denied another victim, and all that – but I still hope she does not do it. It might start Dad off. He is not as reserved as people think. I remember him crying when Nobby Stiles took out his false teeth after the 1966 World Cup – I mean, of course, when Nobby Stiles took out his *own* false teeth. He never had a go at Dad's – though I wouldn't have put it past him if Dad had looked like scoring. Then again, when Bambi's mother copped it in the film of the same name. You couldn't blame him for that. I don't reckon anyone could sit through that and not start feeling for something to blow his nose on – that is what I told Carol Farmer at the time, anyway, though she still had me thrown out of the cinema. She was a funny girl. Her right hand never knew what her left hand was doing and always seemed surprised to find out.

I press the front door bell and listen to the silence. Dad brought home a Multi-Vibe Temple Chime from the lost property office where he goes to sleep during the day but he has clearly not got around to fixing it up yet. Wait a minute! I tell a lie. There, nailed to one of the peeling door jambs is the aforementioned M-V TC looking like a rusty xylophone. Beside it hangs a mallet. I can imagine the whole thing appealing to Dad's sense of refinement and grandeur. Although a convicted socialist – I have never been able to find out what all the convictions were for – he nicks *Country Life* from the doctor's and on one occasion even made a toilet paper holder out of a cover. He would get an upper class thrill out of wiping his bum on the contents pages if they were not so shiny.

Feeling like the geezer who bashes the gong at the start of those old J Arthur movies I have a go at the Temple Chime and step smartly to one side as it crashes to the ground. Hardly has the first note rung out and the third piece of piping bounced half way across the street than the front door bursts open and I find myself face to face with Dad. His bloodshot eyes gaze deep into mine and I see a look of haunted anguish that makes my worst fears come true. Here is a man living on the very edge of reason. A man practically unhinged by the return of a well-loved child given up for lost. 'Dad!' I say, throwing my arms around him.

'Get off me, you git-faced twit!!' shouts my father. 'Have you gone round the twist? Look what you've done. Do you know how much those things cost in the shops? Oh my Gawd!'

So saying, he casts himself on the ground and begins trying to retrieve pieces of the Temple Chime. Much as the thought distresses me, it is clear that its multi-vibes will never again be harnessed into one glorious ringing note.

'I'm all right, Dad,' I say, comfortingly.

'You're all right?' screams Dad. 'Who told you that? Let me know and I'll have him certified. You're not all right! You're the most destructive little sod that ever drew breath and unemployment benefit.'

'Dad! Please!' I say. 'Think of your heart.'

Dad shakes his head. 'Every time I look at you, I wish I'd listened to your mother.'

'Why Dad? What did she say?'

'She told me to stop it!' says Dad bitterly.

Before I can decide whether to question Dad more closely on this delicate subject, Mum appears carrying a dustpan and brush. She, at least, looks as if she has got her feelings under control. It is strange, but I have often noticed how women, who are supposed to be the weaker sex, can often show tremendous resolution in times of stress.

'It's fallen down again, has it?' says Mum. 'I told you it should have been fixed up properly. You ought to have got an electrician in.'

'I'm back, Mum,' I say.

'I'm not made of bleeding money,' says Dad. 'Those blokes cost a fortune. It would have been quite all right if clumsy clot here hadn't laid his lazy, no good hands on it.'

'I'm back, Mum,' I repeat. 'From the snowdrift.'

'You can't blame him, Walter,' says Mum. 'The milkman had it down as well. It shouldn't be hanging there, that's the long and short of it.'

'From the snowdrift on the desolate Pennine Hills,' I say. 'Mickle Fell.'

'My bleeding door chimes fell, and all!' says Dad. 'What's the matter with you? Why can't you think of other people for a change?'

I am beginning to understand that concern for his door chimes has temporarily blinded my father to my absence. It is sad but not totally unexpected. I swallow my disappointment and turn to my mother. 'Mum,' I say. 'I don't wish to appear melodramatic but I have been lost for two nights in one of the worst blizzards the north of England has known. Have you at any time during that period experienced any feelings of what I might describe as unease?' I watch my mother's face consider the question for a moment and then shape itself into an expression of extreme distress. Perhaps I was too blunt.

'Oh!' she says. 'Oh, no!!'

Immediately, I feel guilt-stricken. I should have bided my time; let her come to terms with my return in her own way. 'I'm sorry, Mum,' I say. 'I didn't mean—'

'What's the matter now?' says Dad peevishly.

'His supper's been in the oven for three days,' says Mum.

I would not mind so much if she did not still expect me to eat it! I mean, I never reckoned her corn beef fritters much at the best of times. After three days in the oven they taste like coke butties. One thing I will say for them, they don't crumble in your pocket – they rip the lining to pieces but they don't crumble. I smuggle two out and I can't force them between the bars of the drain they are so tough.

One thing I am surprised to learn, when Dad has stopped fretting about his chimes, is that we have been invited to supper by sister Rosie and brother-in-law, Sid. Not only supper but during a weekday, too. What is more, Rosie refers to the meal as dinner and thoroughly confuses everybody. Dad does put in a token appearance at the lost property office, most days, to see if there is anything worth nicking and Mum is quite likely to be queuing up for her favourite seat at the bingo during what we call dinnertime.

Of course, it turns out that Rosie is being toffee-nosed and referring to supper. She is not the girl she was when we were all living together in Scraggs Lane. The success of the boutiques and wine bars has gone to her head. Now she lives in Vauxhall, or East Westminster as she chooses to call it, she has become all classless and stripped pine. I even saw her with a 'Vote Liberal' sticker on her Fiat. Mum and Dad don't know what to make of her and Sid has his problems. While she has gone from excess to success, he has floundered. None of his recent business ventures has prospered and I reckon that he must have sunk every penny he had in Noggett Transport. My load of glasses being written off could be the last straw. Poor Sid. How am I going to tell him? Well, not while I am by myself for a start. Just in case he turns nasty. It has been known to happen. If I wait till we go to supper then I will have Mum and Dad to back me up, or at least, get in the way if he starts throwing things. Then there is Rosie. She can always be relied upon to side with anyone against Sid. Yes, I will put off the evil moment until the evening.

Mum and Dad are very agitated about the forthcoming event. Dad even takes the day off from work to prepare for it. It is strange because he is always saying what a sponging git-face Sid is, yet, when he gets an invitation to his home, he doesn't want to go.

'We'd better take something, I suppose,' says Mum.

'Yeah, bicarbonate of soda,' says Dad.

'What do you mean?' says Mum, all worked up. 'I taught Rosie everything I know about cooking.'

'That's what worries me,' says Dad.

Mum looks at him coldly. 'I was referring to a gift. You have to take something when you go out to supper with people. It's manners.'

'Well, you buy them something,' says Dad. 'I can't afford to. It seems stupid to me. What's the point of receiving hospitality if you have to pay for it?'

'Some of those mints,' says Mum. 'They'd be nice. I've seen them on the telly.'

'They're not on the telly now,' says Dad.

'I mean, advertised on the telly!' says Mum. 'Really, Walter, I don't know how you hold down that job of yours sometimes.'

Mum keeps on at him and in the end he grumbles off to the newsagents. He is gone a long time so I know that he has been having a browse through the girlie magazines. The way his mince pies have gone all pink gives the game away as well.

'Well, did you get them?' says Mum, looking at his empty hands expectantly.

Dad dives one of his mits into his raincoat pocket and produces a roll of mints. 'Extra strong,' he says proudly.

'I didn't mean them!' screams Mum. 'I meant the wafer thin ones. You can't give those to people!'

'Well I'll have them, then,' says Dad.

By the time six o'clock comes and Mum reckons it is time for us to leave, she is in a right flap. 'Make sure you go to the toilet before we leave, Walter,' she says.

'What are you on about?' says Dad. 'They've got a toilet there, haven't they?'

'Yes, but I'd rather you used this one. I know what you're like!'

'Mum, please!' I say. 'Do you have to? It's so embarrassing.'

'It's embarrassing for me, too,' says Mum. 'I have to clean up after him.'

'I don't know why we have to leave now,' says Dad. 'It's not going to take us two hours to get there.'

'You never know, with the buses the way they are,' says Mum, pressing shut the studs on her flower-motifed Packy-Macky – it looks like a shower curtain. 'They travel in convoys. If you miss one you can wait for hours.'

'It's them sambos,' says Dad. 'They're all used to living in tribes so they stick together. You never see a white bus conductor, these days.'

'We want to get there a bit early, anyway,' says Mum. 'Eight o'clock is too late for supper. I'm surprised at Rosie.'

'You're right,' says Dad. 'I'll think I'll pop into the kitchen and make a bacon sandwich to tide me over. Do you fancy one, son?'

'Oh no you don't!' says Mum. 'I'm not having you ruining your appetite and getting your fingers all greasy. I want you to do Rosie's meal justice.'

Of course, we end up getting a bus almost immediately

and arriving on Rosie's doorstep just after seven. I know that my sister is not going to be very glad to see us but at least it will give me time to sort out my business with Sid.

It is the man himself who wrenches open the front door. 'Blimey,' he says. 'It's you. I thought it was the food.'

'The food?' says Mum.

'Rosie's having one of her Chinese evenings,' says Sid. 'It's brought up from Limehouse.'

'A lot of it's brought up *in* Limehouse, so I hear,' says Dad. 'Oh dear, I've never been very partial to chink nosh. It comes out the way it goes in if you know what I mean.'

'Walter, please! Don't let's have any of your distasteful remarks at this stage of the evening,' says Mum. 'Well, Sidney. Are we going to be allowed to cross the threshold?'

Sid steps to one side hurriedly. 'Of course, Mum. Come inside. I'll get you a drink.'

'I must have a word with you,' I hiss to Sid.

'Yes I know,' says Sid. 'In a minute.' He follows Mum and Dad into the house, leaving me to wonder how he could have found out my guilty secret so soon.

'Tell them to put it on the table,' shouts my sister's voice from upstairs. 'I wouldn't put it past Mum to roll up in a minute. Anything free has them round faster than—'

'Ah hem!' hollers Sid. 'The family are here, dear. I'm just giving them a drink.'

'I'll be right down!' Rosie's voice changes so that it flows down the stairs like a torrent of treacle.

'What would you like, Mum?' says Sid.

'A sherry would be nice,' says Mum. 'I see you still haven't got the settee covered.'

I knew Mum would pick on that. I have always thought it was strange, myself. I don't know how they can stand that bare leather. It looks so unfinished.

'It's meant to be like that,' says Sid, handing Mum a glass.

'That's not very generous, Sidney,' says Dad. 'You might give your mother-in-law a decent tumblerful. It's not often we're invited here.'

'That's a special sherry glass,' I say. 'You have to have it in that.'

'That's right,' says Mum. 'Don't you know nothing, Walter? I can always have another one.' She hands Sid back her now empty glass. 'Try to develop a little couth, dear.'

'I'm thinking of you, that's what I'm doing,' grumbles Dad. 'You're my wife and I'm standing up for you.'

'You've left it a bit late for that,' sniffs Mum. I am not quite certain what she means by that remark and less than eager to find out.

'What are you having, Dad? Scotch?' says Sid.

'Just a large one,' says Dad, looking round the room, eager to see everyone laughing at his joke.

'Why do you always have to say that, Walter?' says Mum. 'Why can't you think of something original?'

'Being offered a scotch by this geezer is original enough for one evening,' says Dad.

'I'll have a scotch, too,' I say.

'I've got some light ale in for you.' Sid nods towards a crate in the corner.

'No thanks, I'll still have the scotch.' I would rather have the light ale but I don't like the thought of having such unsociable tastes that they have to be specially catered for. I remember how Dad used to grumble about getting a bottle of peppermint cordial in for Gran when she used to spend Christmas with us. I expect she misses it where she has gone.

Sid catches my eye. 'It's a disaster, isn't it?' I think he

is talking about this evening and nod. 'At least she got out alive, that's the main thing.'

'You could look at it like that,' I say – reckoning that he is talking about my ordeal in the snow. Frankly, his words puzzle me. Having first hand experience of Shirl's insatiable appetites I would say that it was I and the other bloke who were lucky to get out alive. Shirl's survival potential was never in doubt.

'I mean, what's a lorry compared to a human life?'

What is Sid on about? There is nothing wrong with Enid. It occurs to me that he may be talking about something else. That would account for him not having thumped me round the earhole the minute I came through the door. Perhaps he doesn't know anything about the broken glasses. 'Sid—' I begin.

'I must have nudged it out of gear with my backside,' he says. 'I'd put the hand brake on I'll swear to it. I got my head up for a second and there it was, slipping backwards.'

'Your head?' I say.

'No, you berk. The lorry. Thank goodness she could swim.' Sid shakes his bonce. 'Oh, I shudder every time I think about it.'

'Sid,' I say. 'I think you imagine I know more than I do. Are you telling me that you were farting about with some bird in the cab of your lorry and managed to shunt the whole bleeding issue into the drink?'

'Drink?' says Dad. 'Your mother and I wouldn't say no. What are you two talking about?'

'Where's Rosie?' says Mum. 'She is expecting us, isn't she? I want to see the children.'

'Go up if you like,' says Sid. 'She won't mind. She's just putting on her cheong san.'

'Caught her at the awkward time of the month, have we?' says Mum. 'Never mind. I'll pop up and say goodnight to the children. How is Jerome's bite?'

'Very painful,' says Sid. 'Make sure he doesn't get the chance to give you one.' He pours Dad another scotch and turns back to me. 'I thought you knew,' he says. 'It was in the papers.'

'I didn't see any papers where I was,' I tell him. 'Sid, this is terrible. Is the lorry all right?'

'I don't know,' says Sid. 'Since it sunk to the bottom of the Thames I haven't seen it.'

'Gordon Bennett!' I say. 'How did the bird take it?'

'In the normal way,' says Sid. 'As I recall it her feet were wedged against the dashboard and I was—'

'I didn't mean that!' I say. Honestly, Sid is about as sensitive as a cast-iron sheath. 'How did she react to such an awful experience?'

Sid closes his eyes and winces. 'The whole thing was horrible. Screaming, fighting, struggling! I can hardly bear to think about it.'

'But she came round in the end, did she?'

'That wasn't her, that was me!' says Sid. 'If it hadn't been for her I wouldn't be here now. She dragged me ashore with her teeth – my teeth as well, we didn't lose anything.'

'Except the lorry,' I say, grimly. 'At least it makes it easier to tell you my bad news.'

I tell Sid about the glasses and he buries his face in his hands. 'That's it!' he says. 'We're ruined. Not to put too fine a point on it, we're up shit creek without a paddle – in fact we don't even have a bleeding canoe!'

It is perhaps fortunate that at that moment Mum and Rosie start to come down stairs.

Dad takes one look at Rosie and puts down his glass. 'Blimey, girl!' he says. 'Have you seen that dress you're wearing?'

'Of course I have,' says Rosie. 'I didn't put it on in the dark.'

'It's new, is it?' says Dad.

'It is actually,' says Rosie. 'Don't you like it?'

'You want to take it back!' says Dad. 'It's got a bleeding great slit up the side. Anyone can see straight up to your fundaments!'

'Oh Dad!' Rosie bites her lip in exasperation. 'You never change, do you? It's *supposed* to have a slit up the side. That's the way the Chinese wear them. It goes with the evening, don't you see?'

'That's right, dear,' says Mum. 'You've seen it on the telly. You remember that film with William Holden, "The World of Suzie Wong"?'

'He didn't wear one, did he?' says Dad. 'I thought I hadn't seen much of him lately. That explains it.'

Before there can be any more explanations, the front doorbell rings. 'That'll probably be the food,' says Rosie. 'Show them in, Sidney, will you? I'll help myself to a drink. It's the only way I'll get one.'

'I wouldn't mind another little drop,' says Mum, putting down her sherry glass and picking up a tumbler.

'Me neither,' says Dad.

I can't help noticing that Mum and Dad are knocking back the booze like there is a prize for it. I do hope that this is not going to lead to any unpleasantness later in the evening.

As Rosie deals with the drinks, the door opens and a really knock-out bird sails in. She is wearing a long black dress that hangs down from just beneath her knockers and touches the floor, and her blonde barnet flops beguilingly over one eye. Dad registers the newcomer and it is easy to see that he is impressed.

'Blimey very muchee,' he says. 'You no lookee likee Chinese lady.'

Rosie looks embarrassed. 'This is Imogen Fletcher, father,' she says.

'No soundee like Chinese lady,' says Dad.

'I no am Chinese lady, that's why,' says the bird in a very upper class drawl. 'My husband and I have lived at Stockwell for three and a half years now. We're practically natives.'

'You're not like most of the natives you see round here,' says Dad. 'Do you want a hand with the grub? I hope you don't expect me to eat with those joss sticks. I have enough trouble with a spoon. I find the bean shoots get stuck between my dentures. Do you have— ?'

Listening to Dad is like wanting to cry out when you are having a nightmare. You can see all the terrible things that are happening but when you open your mouth, nothing comes out. Fortunately, Rosie does not have my problems when it comes to basic communication.

'Really, father!' she says. 'How can you be so stupid? Surely it's obvious that Imogen and Crispin have nothing to do with the meal. They're guests, like you.'

It occurs to me that Imogen is not a guest like Dad, and Crispin, when he comes into the room bears even less resemblance to my father – or anyone else's father for that matter. He is wearing a kind of silk tank top with puff shoulders and sleeves and a chiffon scarf that comes down to his knee breeches. These are fastened by a diamanté buckle as are his black shiny shoes. It is a dead cert that he is not a New Zealand rugby player.

He stops in front of Dad and claps his hands together.

'How quaint!' he says. 'I've never seen it done better.'

'Your friends may be able to say the same about you,' says Dad menacingly. 'What are you on about?'

'Look at those clothes, darling,' pipes Crispin. 'They're

so authentic, aren't they? I wonder if his trousers are held up with string?'

'Crispin's terribly well known as an interior decorator,' explains Rosie.

This news does not surprise me. I have no difficulty at all in imagining the creep decorating interiors. What does surprise me is that Rosie should fancy someone like that. It is because he is artistic, I suppose. She always reckons that she is a bit starved in that direction having Sid as a husband.

Crispin is still staring at Dad's suit. 'Where did you get it from?' he croons. 'Do you have pull at the Salvation Army?'

Actually, I think Crispin is being a bit unkind. Dad's best suit is no worse than any other old geezer's clobber. The stains round the front of the trousers aren't very nice but the half inch of grey woollen underpant protruding above the belt and giving way to the frayed ends of the waistcoat dangling temptingly above it seems to have been with me since childhood. Maybe that is it. I am too used to Dad. Either that, or his cap is creating the wrong impression. I saw Mum trying to take it off him when they came through the front door but he wasn't having any.

'And that lovely dress,' says Mrs Fletcher, turning to Mum. 'Did you knit it yourself?'

'No,' says Mum with a funny half curtsey – I can understand why she does it. Imogen Fletcher does make you think that you are in the presence of royalty – 'I got it at Marks and Spencers. I get all my stuff there. All my clothes that is.'

'They are marvellous, aren't they?' says Mrs F brightly. 'I noticed they had avocados there the other day.'

'Oh really?' says Mum. 'That is nice.'

'What would you fancy to drink?' says Sid.

Mrs Fletcher orders and turns to me. 'You must be young Timothy,' she says. 'I've heard so much about you.'

'Nothing too terrible, I hope,' I simper. Mrs Fletcher is the kind of poised upper-class bird who reduces me to a shapeless, mumbling twit. There are tiny little valleys at the corners of her lovely soft cakehole and when she twitches her lips it is as if somebody has pulled a bit of string tied round my Willy Wonker. I nearly ice my birthday cake.

'Quite the reverse,' says the lady. 'I believe you've been a tower of support to Sidders in his many business ventures.'

For a moment, I wonder what she is talking about. Then I get it. She means Sid. The upper classes are always messing about with names, aren't they? Ronny is acceptable but with Ron you have practically kicked the bucket – or gone beyond the pail, as the nobs say.

'I've done what I can,' I say. 'Tell me, how do you know Sid and Rosie?'

Mrs F accepts a drink and gestures me towards the settee. 'It's all to do with Crispin,' she says draping herself gracefully across the scuffed leather. 'He had a hand in your sister's venture.'

I am surprised at her coming out with it just like that but some of these posh bints don't care what they say. That's what makes them so exciting. On the surface all pure and untouchable, underneath raring to cop a snatchful of steaming hampton straight between the thighs. What does come as a bit of a shock is that Crispin is a furburger fan. I had reckoned him as being a bit of a ginger on the noisy. Just shows how you can't make sweeping judgements about people.

'Yes,' continues Mrs F. 'He was in at the start of the boutiques and did all the decor for the wine bars.'

'Oh,' I say as it occurs to me that I may have misunderstood the lady. 'You mean the sawdust and that?'

'Inspirational, wasn't it?' says Mrs Fletcher proudly.

'Definitely,' I say. 'I know that Sid uses a lot of it for the kiddies' ferrets.' I see a look of doubt coming into Imogen's eyes. 'The sawdust, I mean,' I say hurriedly.

'Of yes,' Mrs Fletcher looks round and then places one of her elegant, beautifully manicured Germans on top of mine. 'Do you think you could coax a teensy weensy bit more gin into my glass? I'm a rather greedy girl, I'm afraid.' The way she looks at me when she speaks, I would walk barefoot across a sea of white hot coals to fetch her a Kleenex. I stand up and she touches my jacket. 'Some ice would be fantastic too.' She winks at me and I have fallen in love. To think I was really not looking forward to this evening. The best things always happen when you least expect them.

I have just wrenched the stupid bird-motif measuring device off the top of the gin bottle and poured Imogen Fletcher a generous slug when Sid moves to my side.

'Where's the ice, Sid?' I ask.

'It's in the – fuck!' Everybody stops talking and Sid examines the front of his jacket. He had tipped up the gin bottle without looking at it and copped the rebound from the bottom of the glass he was filling. 'Uxbridge!' shouts Sid, 'Just beyond the traffic lights. You can't miss it.' The threads of conversation are picked up again and Sid turns to me. 'Did you do that, you stupid berk?' he hisses.

'Sorry, Sid,' I say. 'It pours so slow with that thing in it.'

'That's the idea, you prat! Just leave things alone.'

'Just tell me where the ice is,' I plead.

'I didn't get any out – I didn't have time with you arriving an hour early!'

'I'll try the fridge,' I say.

Mrs Fletcher gives me a melting look that would see off

any lump of ice I had in my hand and I sear towards the kitchen. Crispin Fletcher tries to catch my eye as I speed past and, rejected, turns back to Dad. 'That really is very interesting,' I hear him say.

'That's just some of the stuff we get in,' says Dad. 'Then there's walking sticks and shooting sticks and umbrellas – oh yes, we get a lot of umbrellas. The last time we counted he had—'

I whip into the kitchen and close the door behind me. It does not half have a lot of gadgets. When you look around, you can see that Rosie is doing all right. I don't reckon that Sid bought too much of this lot. I have just opened the fridge and knocked a tub of cream over three stories of food when Rosie rushes in.

'It hasn't come!' she storms. 'Little perishers. They promised it by eight.'

'Oh, the food,' I say, cottoning on to what she is rabbiting about. 'Can't you give them a ring?'

'I don't have the number. I called in on the way home.'

'They must be in the book,' I say.

'I can't remember the name. You know what they're like: Hing Pong, Flung Dung – it could be anything.'

'If you had a classified you could find out from the address.'

'But I don't!' Rosie faces me angrily. 'What's the matter with you? Are you an undercover agent for the GPO or something?'

'Calm yourself,' I say. 'We all have our problems. Where's the ice?'

'In the top. Oh no!' Rosie looks inside the fridge. 'Did you spill that?'

'No, it was like that when I opened it.'

'It must have been Sid,' snarls Rosie. 'I'll kill him one of these days!'

'You mustn't be too hard on him,' I say, holding the ice tray under the hot tap. 'He's had a lot on his mind, lately.'

'A lot on it and nothing in it,' spits Rosie. 'I'll have to give them something to tide them over. Don't let Dad have another drink what ever you do. He's pissed already.' She puts a jar marked 'cheese' on the table as I look around for something to put the ice in. 'I'll give them a quick fondue.'

'You'll what?!' I say.

'Give them a fondue – a cheese dip.'

'I thought you said you'd give them a quick fondle!'

I think the misunderstanding is quite funny but Rosie seems to have lost whatever sense of humour she once had. She accuses me of getting in her way and pushes me to one side while she puts on a saucepan. It is all I can do to tip the ice into a jar before she drives me out of the kitchen. When I get back to the lounge, Imogen is sitting where she was but her lovely mince pies shelter a look of reproach.

'I thought you'd forgotten about me,' she says.

'I don't think I could ever forget about you,' I say.

'How nice.' Her lips twitch again like they did last summer and I feel percy preparing for a game of 'Launch My Zeppelin'. 'You got the ice, did you? I'm sorry to be such a terrible nuisance.'

I make a few mumbling noises and hand over her glass. When she looks at me like that it is difficult to think of things to say. I take the top off the jar and hold it out to her. It seems better mannered to let her help herself rather than cop a mitful of my germs. If I had thought about it I could have brought a pair of tongs but it is too late now. She is still holding my glance and I wonder if she knows what is passing through my mind – I hope her husband doesn't. Possibly, she is feeling something of what I feel. Beautiful, mature women of the world do fall passionately in love with simple working class lads like me. Half the plays you turn over to on BBC 2 for the juicy bits are about it.

Mrs Fletcher sticks her mit in the jar and – 'Oh!' We both look down to see that her delicate digits are grasping what looks like a cube of parmesan cheese. Oh my gawd! In my confusion I must have tipped the ice cubes into the cheese jar. 'How frightfully original,' says Mrs F.

Rosie appears at my side. 'You didn't touch the—' She takes a butchers at the object between Imogen's fingers and squeaks.

'I think, if you don't mind—' says the love of my life.

'I'm very sorry,' I say. 'I didn't mean—'

Rosie snatches the jar out of my hand. 'Are you mad?!' she says. 'Are you stark raving mad?'

Before I can say any more, the front door bell rings. 'It must be the nosh – I mean, food,' I say. 'I'll let them in.'

As I head for the door, I hear Rosie explaining that both Sid and I have been under a lot of strain lately. It is noticeable that when she talks to the Fletchers her voice is a lot more refined than it is when she is parleying to the family.

'– a hundred and forty-five with broken spokes. Of course, with them it's touch and go as to whether they were lost or abandoned. That's something only experience will tell you –' Dad's voice is still droning on as I open the front door.

'Solly about delay. Go to wong address. Very tlying.' The little bloke with the pile of containers is behind me before he has finished his sentence. I look out into the street in case there is any one else but there is only a large black cat running as fast as its legs will carry it. 'Where you want?'

'Well, I think everybody's quite hungry now,' says Rosie looking at Dad anxiously. 'Can you lay it out on the table, please?'

'Chinese food? How lovely!' Imogen Fletcher drops the cheese-covered ice cube into an ashtray and rises to her feet.

'Those cats were Kung Fu fighting,' croons Dad. 'I don't reckon it myself, you know. I mean, look at him. He doesn't come up to my chest.'

'Neither does anyone else if they got any sense,' says Mum. 'Come on, Walter. Get a grip on yourself.'

The Chinese bloke is laying out lots of little cardboard boxes full of grub and taking no notice of Dad.

'You hear what I say, Chinky Chops?' goads Dad. 'Show us a bit of the old martial arts. Bamboo stalk that bend in wind no support mighty pagoda. You savvy words of Oriental wisdom?'

'You savvy punch up throat?' says the small Chinese gentleman.

'Stop it, Dad!' says Mum. 'Can't you see you're embarrassing everybody?'

Dad starts swaying and bobbing – he has been swaying for most of the evening. 'Those cats were Kung Fu fighting,' he chants. 'Oh, it was most exciting – Come on, Ping Ling. Show us your muscles!'

The Chinaman places both hands together and bows towards Sid. 'Food laid out,' he says.

'You know what you are?' says Dad. 'You're yellow! All you Chinks are the same. You can't even get a proper Chinaman to play one of you. That bloke in 'Kung Fu', he's not Chinese. They pull his eyes back with sellotape.' WHAM! CRASH! BANG! Dad turns a couple of somersaults – it may have been three, it happens so fast – and lands in an untidy heap on the settee.

The Chinaman gives Sid another bow. 'Honourable gentleman laid out,' he says.

'Do something!' screams Dad, scrambling to his feet and trying to hide behind Mum. 'Don't let him get away with it. Coming in here and assaulting innocent people. Ring for the police!'

'Do shut up, Walter,' says Mum. 'You had it coming to you.'

'Yes, Dad,' says Sid. 'Belt up!'

The Chinaman goes out and Dad immediately advances to the drinks tray and empties the remains of a bottle of brandy into a tumbler. 'Soon saw him off, didn't I?' he says. 'Didn't take him long to see which way the wind was blowing. He could see what was going to happen – one carrotty chop on a vital nerve point and – pouf!' – Crispin looks up sharply. 'All the way back to Gerard Street in a wheelbarrow.'

'Talking of carrotty chops,' says Sid, indicating the nosh. 'We'd better get stuck into this lot before it gets cold.'

In fact, it is cold. And there is not much worse than cold Chinese food – though this stuff would probably run it close when it was hot. Crispin and Imogen send out a series of polite squeaks but Dad is blunt in his attitude to the fare provided. 'I don't mind the vinegar,' he says. 'That's got more taste than the rest of it put together. I reckon it's why they're so small, these Chinks. You can't build a man up on this, can you? It's not like the roast beef of old England.'

'The Roast Beef of Old England doesn't seem to have got us very far at the moment, does it?' says Crispin, carefully picking a bean shoot off his blouse.

'What's that supposed to mean?' says Dad. 'Don't you fancy this country, then? Are you one of those knockers whose always saying we're not the greatest nation living on Earth.'

'We will be living on earth if we go on at this rate,' says Crispin.

'Oh yes, darling. Very good,' says the lovely Imogen.

'What do you mean, very good ?!' says Dad ferociously. 'That's not very good, that's bleeding awful! Are you a foreigner ? Come over here to load yourself up with free specs and dentures on the National Health ?!'

Oh dear. I can see that the demon liquor has once again unhinged Dad's feeble mind. He always becomes unpleasant when he has had a few.

'Dad –!' says Sid.

'Not so much of the Dad, sonny! Your relationship to me is one of marriage not blood. You never sprung from my loins.'

'He would if he had to get anywhere near them,' sniffs Mum.

'You shut your face!' says Dad.

'Really!' bristles Imogen. 'I think you're the most unpleasant old man I've ever met!'

'That's because I'm a patriot!' rants Dad. 'Because I won't stand to see my country run down by shameless hussies who want to show off their tits and inflame men's natural appetites! If you're so proud of them, let's all see them!' So saying, he lunges for the front of Imogen's dress, loses his footing, and collapses on the imitation sheepskin rug.

'That's it!' snaps Rosie. 'I want him out of my house! I don't care if he is my father. I never want to see him again!'

Mum stops hitting Dad over the bonce with her shoe. 'What do you mean if? Of course he's your father! You mind what you're saying, my girl!'

'Out!' screams Rosie. '*Out ! !*'

Imogen Fletcher rises to her feet, her hand draped elegantly against her forehead. 'Please don't disturb your father,' she says. 'I think it's better if I leave. I'm not feeling very well. Crispin –'

'But you can't leave yet,' says Sid. 'You've hardly touched your sweet and sour pork. Anyway, there's something I want to talk to you both about. It's been at the back of my mind for a long time.'

'Well, I think if – er Imogen isn't feeling herself –'

'I wouldn't put it past her,' says Dad from the floor. 'Feeling herself, I mean.'

'Shut up!' Sid kicks Dad in the stomach and it is obvious that the evening is on the verge of boiling over into unpleasantness. 'You stay, Crispin,' begs Sid. 'If Imogen doesn't feel up to it, Timmy can drive her home. It won't take a minute. I've got an idea I want to talk to you about.'

'Er – well?' Crispin looks at Imogen and I can see that he is about as keen to stay as he would be to substitute his cock for a piece of cheese in a rat trap. To my surprise, Imogen seems prepared to look upon the idea with less than total disfavour.

'I'm certain Timothy doesn't want to take me home,' she says – it is my imagination or is that a pout at the corner of that delectable mouth?

'It would be a pleasure,' I say. 'I mean – I wouldn't mind at all.' I tone my response down when I see the way Crispin is looking at me. Wary might be one way of describing it.

'I think, maybe I'd better –'

'That's settled then,' says Sid breezily. 'I hope you feel better soon Imogen. I'm sorry about my father-in-law. He becomes prone to these bouts of over-tiredness.'

There is a lot more 'lovely evening!' and 'don't mention it' while Rosie fetches Imogen's coat. Crispin has grudgingly given me his car keys and is staring at the jumbo-sized brandy Sid has just shoved in his mit. 'The reverse is up and away from you,' he says.

'Your wife knows the – yes, of course, she must do,' I

say, glad that I have prevented myself from asking if Imogen knows the way to her own home.

'I'm ready,' she calls to me from the front door. Her handbag clicks shut like a trap closing on its prey and she delivers a minute flare of the nostrils as she catches my eye. 'Goodnight, Crispin,' she says. 'I'm going to take one of my pills, so I won't be awake when you get home.' Crispin says something sympathetic and blows her a kiss. They don't have a proper Swiss Miss.

'How do you feel?' I say once we are in the car and I am trying to find out how the lights work.

'Tense,' she says. She feels in her bag and brings out a packet of fags. 'Do you use these?'

'No,' I say. I am wondering whether to do any more apologizing for the family. In the circumstances, it seems best to leave the subject alone. It could sound a bit like a German apologizing for Hitler. 'Tell me where you want me to go, will you?'

'Down the end of the street and turn left. It's very near. I could have walked.'

'Better not to, these days.' I say in my best Dixon of Dock Green voice. 'You might bump into a spot of bother.'

'You mean, I might be raped?' She drags in a lungful of smoke and blows it out so hard that I expect it to splinter the windscreen. 'I should be so lucky.'

'There's one or two nutcases about,' I say.

'Lead me to them!' Mrs Fletcher grits her teeth and rakes her finger nails down my thigh. I manage to keep the car off the pavement, but only just. 'Poor Timothy,' says my volatile passenger. 'You must think I'm mad.'

'Of course, I don't,' I say soothingly. 'You're just a bit unsettled, that's all. The cheese on the icecubes and all that.'

'You think it's giving me nightmares?' Imogen laughs.

'Cheese is supposed to give you mightmares, isn't it?'

'You didn't eat any, did you?' I say soothingly.

Lovely Imogen Fletcher brushes some hair from her eye. 'It's often the things you don't have that give the most trouble, isn't it?'

'I suppose it is,' I say. I don't have to get out my crystal balls to see that there is something troubling the lady. Something apart from Dad and the rest of the agrochat. 'Your family wear their hearts on their sleeves, don't they?' She gives a short laugh. 'That father of yours practically wears his parts on his sleeve!'

'I'm sorry,' I say. 'I –'

Imogen touches my sleeve. 'Turn right at the level crossing and it's the third house on the right. 'Don't apologize for your father. At least he comes out with what he thinks. Crispin and I are less honest.'

I take the car round the corner and pull up outside the third house. It is half a large semi-detached, painted white. I notice that they have new dustbins. 'Here we are,' I say.

Imogen pulls her coat across her Manchesters. 'Come in and have a drink,' she says. 'A coffee, something like that.' The way she says it, she sounds as if she means it. 'You weren't particularly enjoying the party, were you?'

'I was enjoying being with you.'

Imogen waves a hand like a conjuror producing a handkerchief from her sleeve. 'If you come in, you'll continue to be with me.'

I hesitate for a moment while I think what her old man is going to say. Is he going to cut up rough if I don't show up in a couple of minutes? Sid and Rosie haven't exactly been responsible for the party of the year, so far. Am I going to put the kibosh on it even further?

'Nobody will notice if you're away for a few minutes.' She is right, of course. When you're pissed – and everybody at Rosie's was pretty pissed – people can disappear for hours and it seems like minutes. I remember when Sid had it off with Gabriella Duke at Sandy Ponder's party. I thought he's only just gone into the karsi, yet, when they broke the door down they were both starkers and she was – it doesn't really matter what she was doing. That has nothing to do with the time element. It didn't half surprise me, though. Mainly because I was younger, I suppose.

'Are you coming?' Love Goddess is getting out of the car and tilting her flawless nut in my direction. It's meeting a bird like this that makes me wish I'd been to Oxford University. It may seem a funny thing to come out with but it's true. It's all a question of communication. You have to have the same terms of reference if you are going to sustain a relationship. I don't mean having money and talking posh. I mean approaching things in the same way. Having the same attitude of mind. If you don't have that in common then you're never going to get much further than humping the sack together. It doesn't normally worry me overmuch. Only sometimes. Very rarely. Occasionally.

'Crispin's lucky,' she says as she opens the front door. 'He's got his work. He finds that fulfilling,' She waits for a moment in the darkness and then turns on the light. 'I need something more.'

When I think about it, it seems that she was waiting for me to do something. She couldn't have been – could she? I mean, if it had been anyone else, I wouldn't have hesitated. But being her, all cool and refined and unattainable, the thought never entered my mind until the moment had gone.

'You get involved in his work, don't you?' I say.

'Only peripherally. I admire it. I give advice when I'm asked for it. But on the whole, Crispin keeps his work to himself. He keeps everything to himself.'

'You don't do anything?'

Mrs Fletcher runs one of her long fingers up my arm. 'Tea or coffee? Oh, or there's some Ovaltine if you'd prefer it?'

'Tea, thanks,' I say. 'If you don't mind me saying so, I think you ought to find something to do. Look at Rosie. You've no idea what she was like when she first married Sid. It wasn't until she got bored and opened a boutique that she really started developing as a person.'

'Developing what?'

The question throws me for a minute. 'Well – er, self confidence and all that kind of thing. I hardly know her now.'

Mrs Fletcher gives another of her short laughs. 'Crispin hardly knows me now. I don't want the situation to get any worse.'

We have gone through to the mod kitchen and Mrs F throws off her coat and gets down to the teapot in a blaze of spotlights. It reminds me of one of those ads in the women's monthly glossies. Birds always seem to be doing the housework in evening dresses.

Some might be surprised by the turn of events but it is amazing how people, especially women, suddenly start telling you their life history after a few moments' acquaintance. I find it difficult to believe my ears sometimes.

'I don't think Crispin is very interested in women,' continues Imogen, reaching for a very ancient-looking biscuit tin – blimey! I hope the biscuits aren't that old. 'Not sexually, I mean. Has your brother-in-law said anything to you about it?'

'What? About your husband? No, why should be?'

'I think Crispin finds him rather attractive.'

'Sid?!' The mind boggles. I never saw Clapham's answer to Paul Newman as a lighthouse for gingers.

'I think it's latent, mind you.'

I look at my watch. 'Yes, it is a bit, isn't it?'

Mrs Fletcher shakes her head and pours the hot water into the pot. 'You probably have no idea what I'm talking about. Your sister's talked to me about you.' The two remarks seem contradictory but I don't say anything. I find that when birds are in this mood it is best to let them do the talking. 'She intimated that you'd led a very protected childhood.'

I am not quite certain what Rosie could have meant by that. Maybe she was referring to the short period I spent giving Her Majesty pleasure at Bentworth Grange. I suppose I was protected then, though I seem to recall the beak saying that he was bent on protecting other people. I reckon he was bent himself, stupid old bleeder! Putting me away for helping in a slum clearance scheme – that's what it was! I swear to this day that I never thought I was stealing when I helped take the lead off that old building. If anything, I was easing the load on the foundations. Of course, it could have been that Rosie was referring to my sexual innocence. It is amazing how your relations can fool themselves. Especially when they are like Rosie – ravers to the bitten end.

'I wouldn't say I was all that protected,' I say. 'Ta.' I accept a cup of tea and Imogen pushes the sugar bowl towards me. 'I have an artificial sweetener,' she says. She smiles when she speaks as if enjoying a private joke. I wonder what she is talking about?

'Come through to the sitting room.' I do as I am told and follow her into a room with a big bay window and a huge circular lantern that goes up and down on a pulley. Some of the bits of sculpture I wouldn't hang Dad's collection of gas masks on, but it's purely a question of taste. It goes to back up what I was saying earlier about terms of reference. 'Is it a problem being a good boy?' she says, patting the sofa beside her.

Now, I know I am going to appear stupid when I say this, but it has never occurred to me up till now that this smashing bird is looking for what I would only be too pleased to give her. I can't reckon that a lovely tart like that could ever fancy me buttering her tea cake. Even now I am not certain.

'I'm not very good,' I say. You don't want to believe everything Rosie tells you. Sisters don't always know, you know.' I try and take a crafty gander at my watch but she notices immediately. She doesn't miss much, this bird.

'Worried about getting back?' she says. 'Don't bother yourself about Crispin. He'll be quite happy talking about false walls or curtain lengths.' It occurs to me that Imogen Fletcher is a lot more worried about Crispin Fletcher than I am. She never stops talking about the bloke.

'I was thinking of Mum and Dad, actually,' I say. 'I expect they'll want to be getting back soon. The last bus goes soon.'

'You're not going to take him on the bus?! Not in that condition?'

'No, I suppose you're right. Sid will have to run us home.'

'Your father delivers a compliment very forceably.' Mrs Fletcher touches the front of her dress thoughtfully.

'Actions speak louder than words with Dad,' I say. 'At least, sometimes they do.'

'At least you know you're wanted.'

'Er – yes,' I gulp.

'You're not just a hollow clothes horse.'

'Er – no.' I gulp – I gulp easily in either direction. Mrs Fletcher takes the cup and saucer from my hand and pushes them under the settee. It is funny her doing that because I have not finished.

'Will you do something for me before you go?' she says.

Take the budgie for a walk? Wash up the tea things? 'Yeah,' I say.

'Kiss me.' My expression obviously shows her how startled I am. 'Kiss me goodnight.' She says it like the motivation will make it easier for me.

'Of course I will.' She turns her head to one side as she tucks her own teacup out of sight and then swings round so that her sensational mouth is hovering before mine. Once again I allow myself to be mesmerised by those dimples and that tonk-tweaking tremble of the roses (rose hips: lips. Ed). She rests a hand lightly against my shoulder and we kiss. And kiss. And kiss. I don't know what the Guinness Book of Records says about kissing – probably nothing, knowing Ross and Truss – but this delicate and highly charged snog is more like a butterfly helping itself to pollen that an old fashioned lip-bashing. Very gentle and very satisfying – and very effective, too. I think I am more aroused by gentle snogging than the swallow-your-neighbour variety. Percy rises like one of those speeded-up films of the life cycle of a cucumber and if I walked out in the street the bulge in my trousers could get me arrested for carrying a deadly weapon. Oh, what a delicious north and south this bird has. It is like kissing a pitless crumpet. Soft and so, so warm. Honestly, it is tinglesville, folks.

While we kiss, her hand is crumpling up the lapel of my denim jacket and it is obvious that there are strong passions stirring beneath the surface – I could certainly lend them something to stir with, as I have already indicated. Not wishing that percy should keep the secret of his infatuation to himself, I pull Mrs Fletcher towards me and turn so that my love cosh is nuzzling her thigh through a couple of layers of unwanted material. If she does not know what is happening then she must reckon that I am smuggling baseball bats.

'Oh!' she says, closing her eyes and showing her teeth as she lets out a long shiver. 'Do you feel it?'

I was about to ask her the same question but I keep quiet and nod my head up and down. 'I think you're very beautiful,' I say.

'Do you?' She sounds really chuffed about the idea.

'Yes.' Nobody in their right mind or my position would say differently, would they?

'I feel guilty about taking advantage of you to satisfy my needs.'

This statement does not surprise me. Birds have always got to go through a short period of self-accusation before they hit the sack with you for the first time. It doesn't usually last long and can be made even shorter if you step in with the right measure of justification. 'You're not taking advantage of me,' I say. 'I'd love to make love to you.' This is something of an understatement as my throbbing muffin-duffer will bear witness.

'But you're Rosie's brother.'

'I'm likely to be somebody's brother,' I say. 'Ooh! You are beautiful!'

I kiss her again and let the palm of my hand plane her thigh. She slips her hand inside my jacket and slides it round my waist so that it rests in the small of my back. Pausing at knee level I start to tug up her long skirt while she hauls my shirt out of my waist-band. We might be working together to raise a curtain. I suppose, in a way, we are. Percy is certainly ready to hog the centre of the stage and after I have made a few preliminary passes along the inside of Imogen's thighs it is obvious that the supporting cast are ready for the entrance of Super Star. There is certainly no danger of anyone drying up. Leaning back against the settee I whip down my zipper and let Show Stopper cop the limelight. Sometimes it is favourite to coax him in from the wings but there are moments when too much finesse can be a waste of time. This is clearly one of them. Imogen shows me the back of her neck before you can say 'Roger Carpenter' and I find myself digging my fingers deep between the cushions on the settee in an effort to keep a grip on myself. 'Oh – no – OH!' I gasp. It is like being plugged into a velvet light socket. Socket and see, is all I can say to those who wish to know more about the experience.

My desperate cries bring Imogen to my lips. 'I'm sorry,' she says. 'I didn't mean to shock you.'

'It's not that,' I say. 'It's – oh, let's get on the carpet!'

The lady is clearly suffering from nunga-hunger, there is no doubt about it. Whipping the lantern down to ground level so that the room is in semi-darkness, she reaches behind her and steps out of her dress in one movement. I don't watch what happens next because I am bent double trying to get my shoes off. Isn't it amazing how your shoe laces always foul up during those romantic moments? When I am next in a position to cop an eyeful of the glorious blonde creature she is stretched out beside the lantern, the pattern of its light tattooed over her naked body. 'Take me!' she moans.

In my present mood of reckless enthusiasm I could easily leave her a couple of feet behind but I control my impetuosity and enter her no faster than I would the last bus home if there was strong competition for places. Now comes the difficult part. To say that I am exceptionally aroused is to put it mildly but I am aware of the golden maxim: 'Easy come, easy no get invited back for a second wack at the crack'. I must control myself. This lady is very, very beautiful and I must make the most of the privilege that Dame Fortune has conferred upon me.

'Oh, lordy, lordy!' she murmurs. 'That's good, that's good!' I get the feeling that this is her first appointment with the groin greyhound for some time, and the way she is clinging on to me lends weight to the thought. Her legs are crossed round the small of my back and I don't think it is just for luck.

'Ride me! Ride me! You beautiful animal,' she says. I try my best and she starts rippling like a crate of strawberry yoghurt on a bumpy conveyor belt. 'Go on! Go on!' The lady is clearly coming to the boil fast. Just as well really, because if I was standing for Parliament instead of you-know-what I would be in danger of losing my deposit.' 'You're winning!! You're winning!! Aaaargh!!!'

Typical, isn't it? Romping past the post and I don't have a bet on myself. I allow myself a similar freedom of expression to that accorded the lady and feel a warm glow of satisfaction and other things explode through my thighs. Fantastic! This is what life is all about. This is – hand on a minute! Never mind about this. What's that?! The sound of a car door slamming in my right earhole? Mrs Fletcher hears it as well and slips out from underneath me faster than a greasy banana skin. She picks up her dress and races to the window showing a turn of speed that I notice women often find in this situation.

'It's Crispin!' she hisses.

'What! How did he get back?'

'Your brother-in-law brought him.'

Trust bleeding Sid to drop me in it! Why the hell couldn't he wait? I glance at my watch. Blimey! Is it that late?

'Get out!' I start to move towards the door. There is the sound of the front door opening. 'Not that way!'

It doesn't take long for the magic to disappear up the

spout, does it? I start to pull on my trousers as Imogen opens a window. 'You can get out here!'

'Imogen! Where are you?' That is Crispin's voice and he sounds a bit uneasy. I don't hang about to recite the farewell speech from Romeo and Juliet but hop up on the window ledge. There are a row of spikes guarding the basement but, with any luck, I should clear them. With any luck. I mean, this is my lucky night, isn't it? 'My shoes –!'

'Jump!' Imogen gives me a helpful bunt up the arse and I leap into space.

It is wonderful what a few iron spikes can do for your high jump potential. I practically land in the gutter. No sooner have I checked that everything is in the right place than I cast an eye about to suss out the situation. Sid's Rover is parked behind the Fletcher motor so it seems favourite that I slip into it and hide behind the seat until I am driven away. Fast thinking, but then I am like that. I take a couple of steps towards safety and then freeze. Crispin comes out of the front door and looks straight at me: '– left it in the back seat,' he is saying as his voice tails away. For a second, I consider running for it and then I have an inspiration.

'There you are,' I say as if what I am doing is the most natural thing in the world. 'I couldn't get your car started. I've been trying to find a garage that's still open. It's very difficult round here, isn't it?' I walk towards the Fletcher car and feel in my pocket for the ignition key. For one terrible moment, I think I must have left it in the house. Then my desperate fingers close round it. 'Here are the keys. I'm sorry. I should have rung you, but I didn't want to disturb Mrs Fletcher.' I look towards the bay window. There is no sign of Imogen and the window is closed.

Crispin's face relaxes. 'I'm sorry you had all that trouble,' he says. 'She is a trifle temperamental, sometimes. I'll have a look at her tomorrow.'

Sid glances at my feet and waves me round behind the Rover. 'You never know,' he says to Fletcher. 'You may find she starts first time in the morning.'

CHAPTER TWO

In which Timmy and Sid begin to work for interior decorator, Crispin, and encounter a series of mounting problems when they remove a 'false' wall for wealthy Mrs Murdstone.

'Well you nearly messed that lot up, didn't you?' says Sid. 'Bleeding good job your flare bottoms pull off over your head otherwise he'd have seen your feet. I still can't understand why he didn't notice the niff.'

Fletcherville is disappearing behind my right shoulder and I hope that Sid is taking me home. 'Hang on a minute,' I say. 'You did the messing up. Why did you want to come rushing round and spoil everything? Mrs Fletcher and I were just beginning to get acquainted.'

'Oh yeah?' says Sid. 'I hope she sends your shoes back to you.'

'You never know your luck,' I say. 'Come on. You haven't answered my question.'

'I wanted to get Crispin alone, didn't I?' says Sid. 'Fat chance there was with your Dad throwing up in the coal bucket and Rosie doing her nut.'

'Oh yes,' I say. After Imogen's comment about her old man's feelings towards Sid, I am not so certain I care for the implications of my brother-in-law's desire to get Crispin Fletcher alone. 'Why, may I ask?'

'Because I wanted to make an approach to him,' says Sid.

'I see,' I say. 'Well, I admire your honesty in coming out

in the open with it. I suppose it will be a weight off Rosie's mind in the long run – a weight off a few other things, as well.'

'I hope so,' says Sid. 'I honestly think that this would be the start of something big.'

'I don't want the sordid details!' I say.

'There's nothing sordid about it,' says Sid. 'Of course, when we set up the business, there may be a –'

'Business?' I say.

'Of course. What did you think I was talking about?'

'Nothing, Sid,' I say. 'Nothing at all.'

'Don't be bloody rude. I'm talking about going into partnership with Crispin, aren't I? We'll do the conversions and all that and he'll do the interior decorating and poncing about.'

'Conversions?' I say. 'I'm not playing bleeding Rugby League Football for you or anyone! Have you seen those blokes? They train by nutting steam rollers!'

'Shut your mouth, you daft custard!' says Sid. 'I'm talking about house conversions, aren't I'?

'House conversions?' The mind boggles.

'Yeah,' says Sid. 'There's a ton of blokes who need a little job doing round the house but get choked off waiting for a builder to take any notice of them or pissed off at the price he asks for the job. Most of your builders only want to know about building a fleet of bungalows or a block of high rise flats. You could make a fortune going round putting in the things they leave out.'

'You could if you knew anything about it,' I say. 'Since when have you had any qualifications?'

'You don't need them,' says Sid. 'I mean, if a load of micks can build a motorway we're not going to have any trouble dividing up some old biddy's sitting room, are we?'

'But you've got to have some technical knowledge!' I say.

'Of course you have,' says Sid. 'I'm not denying it. I've been accumulating quite a bit lately.'

'Night classes?' I say.

'No, watching them knock down old buildings. You can learn quite a lot by doing that. Where the beams and joists are and all that kind of thing. Did you know that one chimney serves three fireplaces? I thought that each one was attached to an individual fireplace.'

'Amazing,' I say. 'So, on the strength of your observations, we're going to start ripping people's houses apart?'

'I made some notes,' says Sid defensively. 'They're on the back of a fag packet. I hope I didn't throw it away.'

'You want to watch that someone doesn't throw you away,' I say.

'It's not all going to be heavy stuff,' says Sid. 'A lot of it will be wallpapering and that kind of caper. Crispin will specify the materials and we'll put them up. With his creative fee we're going to make a fortune. We're just the back-up he needs.'

'Speak for yourself,' I say. 'You know he fancies you, don't you?'

Sid turns pink. 'What do you mean?'

'His old lady told me. She reckons he's a borderline ginger. Hasn't quite got into his stride, yet.'

'Well, calm yourself. He's not getting into my strides!' Sid tightens his grip on the driving wheel. 'Just because he admires certain aspects of my life style it doesn't mean he's a raving poufdah. A friendship between two men can be a beautiful thing, Timmo. Especially if you stand to make a few bob out of it. What Crispin gets up to when he takes his embroidery round to the Turkish baths, I neither know nor care.'

'I still don't see how it's going to work,' I say.

'You never understand how anything's going to work!'

says Sid bitterly. 'You're a blooming pessimist, that's what you are!'

'Not without some reason,' I remind him. 'Our track record isn't exactly Hall of Famc material, is it?'

'We've been crippled by a capital commitment, that's why,' says Sid. 'Too much money tied up in plant.'

'I didn't know you were running a market garden on the side,' I say. 'I always wondered why your hands were so dirty.'

'I'll give you the benefit of the doubt and assume that was an attempt at humour,' says Sid. 'I'm talking about overheads, aren't I? – and if you mention clouds, I'll smash your face in. The trouble with the road haulage business was that we had all that money tied up in the lorries. It's not a mistake I'm going to be in the position to make again.'

'Because of your heightened perception of the factors affecting the deployment of available assets?' I ask.

'Because I'm skint!' says Sid. 'The only face I possess is the one on my shoulders.'

"That's awful – I mean, your predicament is awful,' I say.

'Yes and no,' says Sid. 'In this sort of situation you've got to be sophistical. I'm poor in moola but rich in experience. What's happened over the last few years has taught me a lot. If you're starting a business, Timmo, never use your own money. Always borrow it. That way, when you go bust, some other poor bastard cops it. Also, don't go in for something that requires a lot of capital equipment. If you have a bomb site and you build a factory on it to make transistor radios, the capital outlay is fantastic and you'll probably find that the Nips have undercut your price by half before you've settled the demarcation dispute with the forty-seven different unions all of whom are on strike anyway. If you turn the bomb site into a car park, you wouldn't have to lay out any cash and you'd be making money from day one with no sweat.'

'That's great!' I say. 'Let's get ourselves a bomb site.'

'They've all gone,' says Sid. 'You'll have to wait for the next war and move sharpish. Getting in with Crispin is the best I can manage at the moment. He's going to pay for our tools.'

'That sounds interesting,' I say.

'You've got a one-track mind,' says Sid. 'And talking of that, you'd better watch it where Mrs Fletcher is concerned. There's nothing so unsettling to a business relationship as finding that one of your partners is doing press-ups on your old lady.'

'You're a fine one to talk!' I say. 'What about Liz? Do you remember her, when we were cleaning windows? We were practically engaged until you messed everything up.'

'Just goes to show you,' says Sid. 'I know what I'm talking about. I've learned from your bitter experience. You ought to try and do the same. Anyway, as far as Liz was concerned, I was just trying to show you that she wasn't right for you. You have to be cruel to be kind sometimes.'

Despite what Sid says, I am determined to see Imogen Fletcher again. I want my shoes back, for one thing. I am also more than a little smitten. It will take me a long time to forget that formidable bout of in and out, accompanied as it was by all the romantic overtones – plus the fact that everything seems better when you are pissed.

Sid is mad keen on his new venture and promptly sets out to flog Enid, that being the only remaining member of the Noggett Transport fleet and his only asset – apart from terminal optimism. He takes her back to Square-Deal Motors and is informed that the incredible demand for lorries at the time when he bought the vehicle has now changed dramatically so that there is a glut of lorries on the market and nobody wanting to buy them. This in turn means that Mr Square-Deal is doing Sid a favour by taking the vehicle off his hands and finding parking space for it. Any price higher than one fifth of what Sid paid for the lorry is out of the question.

When Sid comes round to Scraggs Lane, his grim face is looking even grimmer than usual. 'This is it, Timmo,' he says. 'We're right back to where we started. The money I've got here is hardly enough to buy us a set of tools – in fact, I think I'll buy a jemmy just in case we come really unstuck.'

'What do we do?' I say.

'We wait for the word from Crispin,' says Sid. 'He's got so much on his plate he doesn't know what to do with it. When the right kind of job comes up, he'll introduce us to do the physical alterations. He'll lay down the colour scheme and all that.'

'There's a few jobs need doing around here,' says Mum. 'That doorbell for a start. Your father's taken the loss of his chimes very hard.'

'He'd have lost his chimes a long time ago if I'd had anything to do with it!' says Sid savagely. 'I'd have played "The Dance of the Sugar Plum Fairy" on them with a tent mallet.'

'I don't know what you're talking about,' says Mum. 'I'm suggesting that you might like to fix that doorbell.'

'That's electrical, isn't it?' I say.

'Yeah, but it's probably dead simple, says Sid. 'I think one of Jason's kiddies' encyclopaedias shows you how to do it. You shouldn't have any problem.'

'*I* shouldn't have any problem?' I say.

'Definitely,' says Sid. 'You've got to be able to do these things so that it becomes second nature.'

'What about you?' I say.

'I'm a broad concept man,' says Sid. 'I can't become embossed in too much detail. I've got to see the whole picture.'

'That reminds me,' says Mum. 'I'll miss the start of "Spring in Park Lane" if I don't get a move on. Ooh, I love those Anna Neagle films. She was so refined, wasn't she?'

'I used to prefer Michael Wilding,' says Sid. 'Is that all right, Timmo? Can I safely leave everything in your incompetent hands?'

'Then there's the washer on the bathroom tap,' says Mum, switching on the telly. 'That's been dripping for so long it's worn away the enamel.'

'That's Timmy having a wee wee when Dad's locked himself in the karsi for the afternoon,' says Sid.

'Sidney! What a terrible thing to say!' Anna Neagle's mug has just appeared on the screen and Mum turns the set off immediately as if to spare her suffering.

'I'm not a blooming plumber, you know,' I say.

'I know you're not,' says Sid. 'You're a plumber's mate until you get the experience. When you've finished around here, we'll see if you deserve to be promoted.'

I am sorry to have to say that Mum never gets to see the whole of 'Spring in Park Lane'. The first interruption occurs when I get confused about which way I am supposed to be twisting the bathroom tap and the whole bleeding issue comes off in my wrench. I suppose I should have checked where the stop cock was before I started out. It certainly does splash about a bit once it hits the ceiling. Mum gives me a hand to lash a towel round the mangled pipe end and I get on with the front doorbell while we wait for the plumber. It is just as well that he arrives when he does as it gives Mum and me something to watch while we wait for the electrician – yes, I have a little accident when I am trying to connect these pieces of coloured wire to the right screws. They are confusing, aren't they? And so fiddly, too. It is not surprising that people have accidents.

The one thing that the whole unpleasant experience teaches me, is that Sid is right. There is an opening for a switched-on, technically knowledgeable Jack of all trades. The only problem is that I don't think that I am that bloke.

When Sid sees the results of my labours he is prepared to agree with me. 'We'll have to hire specialist skills when we need them,' he says. 'I've got this Indian carpenter bloke lined up. I hear he's very good if you like the Taj Mahal.'

'That's that curry place in the High Street, isn't it?' I say. 'He did that, did he? I must say, I never thought it was anything special.'

Sid screws up his face. 'I was referring to the original Taj Mahal, wasn't I? One of the most spirit-enriching examples of Indian architecture, built by Shah Jehan to the memory of a dearly beloved wife.'

'Who was she married to?'

'To him, you berk! To him! Really, Timmo, your cynicism about the marital state is very disturbing. I don't know where you get it from.'

Just as well, I think to myself. 'Sorry, Sid,' I say. 'I'm certain this Shah bloke will be very useful. It's just that I haven't got used to the idea of them doing anything else except sitting on elephants waiting for the rains to come. I suppose it's all the fault of Kipling.'

'Kipling?' says Sid.

'Yes, Kipling. You know all about Kipling, don't you Sid?'

'Is it another word for jerking yourself off?' says Sid.

A couple of days later, Crispin gives Sid a ring and they

announce their engagement – no, just my little joke. He gives Sid a ring and tells us to report to one of the houses on the west side of Clapham Common. I am expecting something pretty posh and I am not disappointed. It is semi-detached but enormous. The kind of place you would expect to find broken up into self-contained flats. In fact, as Crispin tells us, this is not the case. 'You'll have to be wary of Miss Murdstone,' he says. 'She's a bit of a martinet.'

'Likes the bottle, does she?' says Sid. 'A lot of the old ones do, don't they?'

'Never touches the stuff,' says Crispin, plucking at his bright green cravat. 'She's teetotally inimical to any form of alcoholic imbibation.'

'Oh,' says Sid. 'That can be the case as well, of course.'

'Her sister has just died and left her a very wealthy woman.'

'I wish somebody would leave me a very wealthy woman,' I say.

'Shut up!' says Sid.

'She's thinking of having the house redecorated from top to bottom. It could be a very sizable contract.'

'Great!' says Sid, rubbing his hands together. 'Let's get at it!'

'Just a word of warning,' says Crispin. 'She's not an easy woman to get on with. If I do all the talking and pass on the instructions for you to jot down, I think that this could pay dividends. It would make everything look more professional somehow.'

'Say no more,' says Sid, tapping his nose. 'Your word is our command, eh?'

'Right,' says Crispin. 'And I think it would be a good idea if we spruced ourselves up a bit. Make sure the old boots aren't dirty and all that kind of thing.'

Beside the front door is an old-fashioned shoe-cleaning gadget made up of two circular brooms that revolve when a handle is turned. You put your foot on one of the brooms, turn the handle and the mud is brushed off faster than Denis Healey cutting in for the last waltz at an Institute of Directors' Bankruptcy Ball.

'It's blooming stiff,' says Sid.

'Hang on. You hold your foot there and I'll do it.' Ever the helpful Timothy, I take a man-sized pull at the handle and watch Sid's shoe disappear through the brushes.

'You stupid berk!' snaps Sid, wrenching free his stockinged foot.

'You don't have to get it out,' I say. 'If I reverse the brushes –'

'Don't bother!' says Sid contemptuously. He drops to his hands and knees and starts trying to insert his hand between the brushes.

'Sid! You'll get yourself filthy,' I say, 'Let me just –'

Sid thinks that I did it on purpose, I know he does. He never understands how flustered he makes me feel – especially in front of other people. Also, all the cogs get me confused. I don't mean to turn the handle and drive his arm so far through the brushes that he finishes up looking as if he is trying to clean his teeth on one of them.

It is unfortunate, too, that Miss Murdstone should choose that moment to open the door. Her reaction to finding a strange man stretched out on her front doorstep with his nut wedged between the brushes of her shoe-cleaning machine is, not unnaturally, one of surprise. 'What is going on here?' she says. 'Mr Fletcher, please explain yourself!'

'My dear lady,' soothes Crispin. 'I hesitate to try and explain the exact nature of Mr Noggett's predicament. I think the event is best described as an accident.'

'Is the gentleman accident *prone*?' says Miss Murdstone, underlining the last word.

Fletcher's reaction to this little jest could be played behind a TV sit-com as a substitute for audience applause. While he is holding himself off the ground and Sid is scrambling away from it, I take a gander at Miss Murdstone. She has a face like an inverted belly button and a nose that could be the largest two-holed wart in the world. I have watched some bad second features in my time but these are ridiculous.

'Delightful,' says Crispin. 'Quite delightful.'

'Who are these men?' says Miss Murdstone like she is already planning to send cook out for an extra order of rat poison.

'Mr Noggett and – er Mr Lea will be undertaking any conversion work that is necessary,' says Fletcher smoothly. 'I thought it advisable that they came in on the ground floor so to speak.'

'Ho, ho,' says Sid. 'Charming, I'm sure.'

'I'm not so sure,' says Miss Murdstone, coldly. 'However, the choice of artisans is in your own, I hope, capable hands, Mr Fletcher. Come, let us to work.'

'Did you hear that?!' I mutter to Sid as we stumble across the threshold. 'I'm not digging any bleeding wells!'

'She said artisans, not artesians!' scolds Sid. 'I can see the kind of magazines you read when you go to the dentists. You want to try something a bit more educational. There's always a few Observer Colour Magazines buried under the photographic stuff.'

'I always go for the photographic magazines, myself,' I say. 'It's the nearest you get to a bit of tit, isn't it? Naomi greets the dawn with a 1/125 exposure and her left knocker hanging out.'

'Did you get that?' says Sid.

'No, I tried to, but the receptionist saw me tearing it out.'

'I mean, what Crispin is saying!!' hisses Sid. 'For heaven's sake, pay attention!' He turns to Crispin and makes a throat clearing noise. 'Excuse me, could we have that again? My mate is having trouble with his fibre tip.'

'Certainly,' says Crispin. 'I was saying that we'd have the Regency stripes horizontal rather than vertical. I think that will give the room a feeling of bonded intimacy. A kind of Marcel Marceau cage holding in that which is not there in the first place.'

'Put the wallpaper on its side,' says Sid. 'Got that? Good.'

'Won't that make the room seem rather small?' says Miss Murdstone. 'I can't abide little rooms.'

'Not necessarily,' says Crispin mysteriously. He is running his hands over the wall at the far end of the room like he is touching it up. 'Yes, I thought so. You have a false wall here. Built in an age when symmetry was all-important.' He peers out of the window. 'You see how the wing goes off at an angle while this wall is at right angles to the end of the building?'

'Good heavens,' says Miss Murdstone. 'I never noticed that before.' She is clearly impressed and Sid winks at me and nods towards Crispin in a 'we've found ourselves a winner here' gesture.

'If we take that wall down, it will give you a few more feet and open up the room.'

'Yes, yes,' says Miss Winkle-bonce. 'That does seem like a good idea. Do it, do it.'

'Have you got that?' says Sid, turning to me.

'Yes,' I say. 'Remove false wall . . .'

'You want to get yourself a proper pad,' hisses Sid. 'It

looks ridiculous taking down everything on the back of an envelope.'

By the time we get up to the attic, I have covered every inch of that envelope in writing. I start off trying to make a plan of each room but this soon proves impossible as the tidal wave of specifications and materials pours out of Crispin's cakehole. I can see what Imogen meant about him being wed to his vocation. He can hardly tear himself away at the end of our visit. 'Look at him,' says Sid admiringly. 'He's got her eating out of his hand.'

'I wouldn't fancy that,' I say. 'She looks as if she could eat your fingers as well.'

'Don't let's have any of that,' says Sid sternly. 'You're going to have to curb your unfortunate tendency to antagonise people if we're going to get anywhere in this business. All the customers aren't going to look like Gayle Honeychops, you know.'

Before there can be further discussion on the matter, Crispin favours Miss Murdstone with a farewell flash of his Teds and turns to us. 'OK chaps. Did you get all that? I've got one or two other spots of business to follow up, so I suggest you start with the basic structural alterations and we'll polish up on the detail later.'

I am relieved to hear Crispin make his last statement as I am having difficulty understanding anything on my envelope.

'Right,' says Sid. 'Let's get down to it.'

'I have to go out to my bridge club,' says Miss Murdstone. 'Can I safely leave your employees to proceed with the minimum of disturbance and mess?'

I can see that Sid is not very happy about the 'employees' bit but as long as we get some money out of the deal I am not too fussed. Whatever they call me, I always end up doing the same job.

'I wonder what you do at a bridge club?' muses Sid as we get the gear out of the back of the van. 'Swop dentures, I suppose.'

'I wouldn't fancy getting hers,' I say. 'Where do you want to start?'

'Start with that false wall, shall we?' says Sid. 'If we get that down nice and tidy, the old girl should be well pleased.'

We both incline our heads as Miss Murdstone drives past down the drive. I notice that she has a 'Bring Back The Cat' sign on her rear window.

'Doesn't look like an animal lover, does she?' says Sid. Sometimes, I don't know whether he is joking or not. We go into the house and Sid turns to me. 'Right, you've got the plan. Where is it?'

'Er – blimey. There's so many doors, aren't there? I think –'

'It's in here,' says Sid, flinging open a door.

'I don't think so,' I say, replacing the vacuum cleaner that has fallen down. 'It was a bit bigger than that.'

Sid closes the cupboard door and grits his teeth like he is trying to crack a walnut with them. 'Don't try and be funny with me,' he says.

I open another door and stick my head inside. 'Was this the one? They all look alike with that antique furniture.'

'Course it was, you berk!' snaps Sid. 'I recognise the candleharbour.'

I take a gander at my envelope but it doesn't help any. 'Lovely wallpaper, isn't it?' I say. 'I reckon it's thicker than the walls back home. Seems a shame to have it down, really.'

'We'll be putting up a new lot,' says Sid. 'Don't start getting sentimental for gawd's sake.'

I tap the wall. 'That's funny. It sounded hollow when Crispin did it.'

'That's because he's got the knack,' says Sid. 'It's like water divining. You and I could hold one of those little sticks over the Atlantic Ocean and we wouldn't get a wiggle.'

'I suppose you're right,' I say. 'Well, here we go.'

'Hang on a minute!' Sid grabs my pick as it passes my earhole on the back swing. 'We've got to put down some dust sheets, haven't we? You remember what the old girl said about making a mess. We don't want to start off by creating a bad impression.'

'You're right, Sid,' I say. 'You do well to castigate me.'

'The thought has flashed through my mind on a number of occasions,' says Sid. 'There's nothing in the van, is there? We'd better have a look round.'

But though we have a very thorough shufti, we don't find anything resembling a dust sheet. 'We could take some of the sheets off the bed,' says Sid. 'They're not going to get very dirty.'

'Better not,' I say. 'Just in case we have an accident.'

'You're right,' says Sid. 'We don't want to take any chances. Tell you what. We'll peel back the carpet so that we don't get it dirty and it's easier to clear up afterwards.'

'Good thinking, Sid,' I say, Sido's business-like approach has got through to me and I am feeling almost enthusiastic as we whip back the carpet.

'Wait a minute,' says my dynamic brother-in-law. 'I've got an even better idea. This floorboard's a bit loose. We'll have it up and sweep everything out of sight, nice and tidy. Give us that pick a moment.'

Sid prises up the board and there is a very handy cavity underneath. 'Right,' I say, taking the pick. 'All systems go.'

'Mind how you swing that thing,' says Sid. 'If it's a false wall it will probably collapse with a couple of bashes. Better let me have a go.'

I stand back respectfully and Sid spits on his hands and grabs the pickaxe like a real pro. 'The whole nack is to get the swing right,' he says. 'Don't hurl yourself at it. Just back and – ooooooh!!'

Sid wings at the wall and the point of the pick bounces back like it has hit steel plating. The vibration passes through Sid's arms and dies out just above his knees.

'Tough, is it?' I say.

'You're not kidding! By the cringe, they knew how to build a false wall in those days. It's just like the real thing.'

'They were craftsmen, then, weren't they?' I say. 'Mum always reckons so, anyway.'

'It was all right for them,' says Sid. 'They didn't have to knock them down, did they? Here, you have a go.' Sid pushes the pick at me and starts massaging his mits. It certainly is tough, there is no doubt about it. I take a couple of swipes and hardly make a dent.

'Hang on a minute,' says Sid, 'Do you hear anything?'

'Blimey!' I say. 'It sounds like somebody knocking from the other side of the wall.'

'There can't be anyone behind a false wall,' says Sid. 'Unless –'

'You mean?'

'That's right,' says Sid. 'Unless there's somebody bricked up behind there.'

'Strewth!' I say. 'It's like that story.'

'It's like all those stories,' says Sid. 'Thank God we were here. Listen to that poor devil trying to attract our attention.' The sound of banging is now becoming almost frenzied. 'Hang on, mate. Relief is at hand.' Sid starts battering away at the wall like a madman.

'Who do you think it is?' I say.

'Could be the old bag's sister, couldn't it? That's how she came into the money. Bricked her up and said she'd snuffed it.'

'It's usually a lover in the stories,' I say.

'I don't reckon it,' says Sid. 'Not with a mug like that. Even your dad wouldn't have a go at that.'

'Might be the sister's lover,' I say.

'Might be the two of them,' says Sid. 'There's enough noise, isn't there?'

'They don't sound too weak,' I say.

'Probably a last desperate frenzy before the oxygen gives out,' gasps Sid. 'Come on, you have a go. I'm knackered.'

Sid has done a good job in the last couple of minutes but we still haven't got through the wall. 'I wondered why it was so thick,' I pant. 'Now it's obvious, isn't it? What a terrible way to incarcerate somebody.'

'You don't reckon she's done that as well, do you?' says Sid. 'Blimey, what a diabolical old woman!'

I take another bone-jarring swing and Sid cries out in triumph, 'You're through! I can see a chink of light.'

'A chink of light?' I say.

Sid applies his cakehole to the scene of the action. 'Stand back, missus!' he shouts. 'We'll have you out in a jiffey.' From behind the wall I can hear muffled shouts and what sounds like somebody swearing viciously.

'She's beside herself,' says Sid. 'Give us that pick. If I can just lever it in this crack – come on, all together! Heave!!'

There is an ominous rumbling noise and an enormous slab of wall falls to the floor – not only to the floor, but through it! It plunges into the gap where the floorboard used to be and disappears from sight accompanied by a sound like someone karate-chopping their way through a stack of wafers. Hardly has it vanished than there is another noise. This time, like a piece of heavy masonry crashing on top of an open piano. I glance through the gaping hole at my feet and – yup! As the cloud of dust clears I can see the stricken piano. The chords are still vibrating.

'We were lucky there, weren't we?' says Sid. 'There could have been a nasty accident. That thing only missed my feet by inches.'

I think that Miss Murdstone could well have a nasty accident when she sees what we have done to her piano. In its present condition, you would be pushed to use it for laying out Christmas cards.

'You dirty rotten scum! You'll never get me out!!'

These do not sound like the words of a woman about to be rescued from a fate worse than death and Sid steps forward to stick his nut through the hole in the wall. He staggers backwards, seconds later, clutching his bonce. 'The woman is round the twist!' he says. 'She's just chucked a brick at me!'

A glance through the hole shows me a woman in late middle age shaking her fist and using the kind of language that you would be pushed to get passed on a BBC 'Play of the Month'. She appears to be sitting in a modestly furnished sitting room. Miss Murdstone can't be too bad. There is even a television set. If she walls you up, she obviously makes it nice for you. What I can't understand is how the space behind the false wall can be so big. Crispin said it was a couple of – oh my gawd!! I look at Sid and Sid looks at me and we are both looking at each other.

'This is the bleeding house next door!' says Sid. 'You started on the wrong wall!'

'You dirty swines!' screeches Miss Murdstone's enraged neighbour. 'You're worse than Rachmann!'

'I wish he was here now,' says Sid. 'Him and his little friend, Robin.'

'She said Rachmann, not Batman, you berk!' I scream. 'Stop her! She's throwing things.'

As if we did not have enough problems, the woman next door is chucking all kinds of rubbish over Miss Murdstone's posh drawing room. 'This is my flat and I'm staying here!' she yells. 'You'll never force me out!'

Sid clears his throat and puts on his most genteel voice. 'Ah hem. Excuse me, modom,' he says. 'You seem to have been the victim of a slight misunderstanding.'

'Slight?!' says the woman. 'I should cocoa. Have you seen the damage you've done?'

'Have no fear,' says Sid. 'We'll make good any damage. Timmo, step through the hole and take down the lady's particulars. I'm nipping out for a bag of cement.'

'If you think you're coming in here, you've got another think coming, mate!' says the lady, accompanying her remark with a neatly aimed half-brick that catches Sid on the side of the bonce.

My bruised brother-in-law draws me to one side and winces as he speaks. 'You'll have to handle this,' he says. 'Promise her anything. We can't afford any trouble at this stage of the game.'

'What are we going to use for money?' I ask.

'We'll use the cash I got for selling your lorry.'

'Can you spare it?'

'I'll take it out of your salary.'

'Thanks Sid.'

'Think nothing of it. Now get in there!'

Sid practically throws me through the hole in the wall.

It is amazing how the thought of losing money gives him the strength of ten – the strength of tenner, in fact.

'You lay a finger on me and I'll scream the place down!' says the old bag.

'Don't worry,' I say. 'If a lay a finger on you – *I'll* scream the place down. Now, let me set your mind at rest. The damage to your property was totally unintentional. My mate and I lost our bearings and started to dismantle the wrong wall. It could have happened to anyone.'

'Round here, it does happen to anyone!' says the woman. 'The property developers are trying to get vacant possession of all the houses. If you're a sitting tenant, they offer you money and if you won't take that, they rough you up or make your life misery. They took the roof off one of my friend's flat. Said it was leaking and that they were going to take it away to check the slates. Five minutes after they'd gone it rained for two weeks.'

'That's not very nice, is it?' I say, soothingly. 'Well, don't worry. You won't have that problem with us. We'll make it good as new. Nice new wallpaper –'

'Where's he going?' interrupts the old girl. She is looking at Sid through the hole in the wall.

'He's going to get the materials to do the job,' I say. 'Hey, Sid, while you're at it, you might as well get the rocks out of the piano.'

'Give us a chance!' complains Sid. 'I've only got four pairs of fingers.'

'I'll go with him,' says the woman. 'I know what I like. You can start cleaning up.'

Before I can say anything she has started scrambling through the hole. 'Careful!' I say. 'There's a –'

I am about to say 'hole' but it is not necessary. Miss Murdstone's neighbour finds it for herself. There is a wild scream and she disappears through the floor. 'Oh my gawd!' shouts Sid. 'Now you've done it.' I would like to query his use of 'you' in the last statement but there isn't time. We race down to the basement and find the unfortunate lady lying on the remains of the wrecked Steinway.

'. . . accompanied on the piano by . . .' I murmur.

'Come to finish me off, have you?!' screams the victim of an unhappy morning's work. 'Murdering bastards! You'd stop at nothing, wouldn't you?'

'My good lady!' says Sid. 'You don't think that was intentional, do you? Oh dear, that's terrible!' He looks round the room and his eyes light on a silver tray with a decanter and some glasses on it. He nods me towards it and starts to help the woman off the piano. Every time she moves, it sounds like Radio Four. I sniff the contents of the decanter and it smells like brandy. Just what the doctor ordered for a serious shock case. I slosh in half a tumblerful and raise it to my lips –

'Not you! Over here!' shouts Sid.

'Rat poison, is it?' says the woman.

'He'd be dead if it was,' says Sid. He takes the glass from me and hands it to the woman. She sniffs suspiciously and – whoosh! You can almost hear her epiglotis vibrating as the booze belts past it down her hairy goat.

'You curl up with this, mother,' says Sid, pushing the decanter into her willing arms and settling her in a convenient armchair. 'We'll go and sort things out and be back later. Don't worry, everything is going to be fine.'

I have my doubts about the truth of Sid's last remark but it seems the wrong moment to say anything. As we go through the door, the old girl is filling her glass again.

'Bastards!' she shouts.

'Is she going to be all right?' I say. 'Hadn't we better get a doctor?'

'She's all right,' says Sid. 'What we need is a piano tuner.'

'What are we going to do?' I say.

'Keep our heads,' says Sid. 'That's vital. "If you can keep your head while all about you are losing their's then you're a man, my son." Surely you've heard that?'

'Something like that,' I say. 'But what about the hole in the wall?'

'Our first problem,' says Sid. 'We've got to fill it in so that Fuzz-face doesn't know that anything has happened.'

'You're mad,' I say. 'What about the wallpaper? Even if we could fill it in, she'd notice that.'

'I've thought of that,' says Sid. 'That room is chocker-block with large pieces of furniture. We'll move one of them, use the wallpaper that's behind it, and move it back again. That thick paper peels off a treat.'

'Then there's the hole in the floor,' I say.

'It's only plaster,' says Sid. 'We'll put the floor board back and tackle that from below.'

'And the piano,' I say.

'I don't reckon anyone ever plays it,' says Sid. 'We'll put a splint on the leg and lay the top back on it – marrying the pieces up as best we can, of course. It'll look as good as new.'

'Sid,' I say. 'Do you really think we're going to get away with it?'

'Naturally,' says Sid. 'There's nothing very complicated is there? The time factor is the only worrying thing.'

When you listen to Sid you can understand how we get stuck with the Concorde, can't you? It only needs a few like him and a couple of dying aircraft industries. We dash back into the room and Sid's eyes rove like a spilt bag of ball bearings. 'That's the one,' he says.

'You mean the enormous sideboard covered in what looks like very rare and expensive plates?'

'Just edge it along the wall a few feet and we'll be in business,' says Sid, cheerfully.

'You don't think it's a bit heavy, do you?'

Sid starts to make 'tch' noises. 'I don't know what's the matter with you today,' he says. 'Everything's too much trouble, isn't it?'

'It's not that, Sid,' I say. 'It's –'

'Come on!' Sid positions himself at one end of the sideboard. 'You pull and I'll push.'

'Watch it,' I say. 'The floor's a bit rotten. If we get one of the casters on a manky bit, it could –'

'Push!' says Sid.

The caster scrapes along the floor for a few inches and then goes through a rotten board like it is a bit of toast. Thrown off balance, the sideboard lurches forward and slowly topples on to its face. There is a loud shattering noise as about thirty plates go for a burton and the whole room shakes.

'Right,' says Sid. 'Now we need some glue as well.'

From the basement come a series of frenzied screams.

'What's she on about?' says Sid.

I walk over to the hole in the floor and look down. Miss Murdstone's neighbour, like most of the room, is covered in a fine pall of dust, no doubt sustained when the sideboard fell over. 'All right! All right!' she screams. 'I'll move! I'll move!'

Outside, there is the sound of a car crunching to a halt on the gravel and Miss Murdstone herself climbs out and starts to move swiftly towards the front door.

'She's back early, isn't she?' says Sid.

'Very,' I say.

Sid looks round the room. 'Well,' he says. 'In the circumstances, I think there's only one thing to do.'

'Exactly, Sid,' I say.

'Thank you, Timmo. Don't forget the pickaxe. We don't want to get a reputation for leaving our tools around.'

I follow Sid through the hole in the wall as the door opens behind me.

CHAPTER THREE

In which Timmy starts by papering Mrs Richmond's walls and ends up being taken advantage of in unusual circumstances.

'I must say,' says Crispin. 'I find it a very distressing start to our relationship.'

'Too true, squire,' says Sid.

I am watching Imogen. Sid, Crispin and I are having what Crispin calls 'a little chat' round at his place and she has just come into the room. *The* room. The room where it all happened. I look at the lantern, now high against the ceiling, and a feel a tender tingle tango down my tonk. Could I actually have had it away with that gorgeous creature? Surely I must have dreamt the whole unforgettable experience? Our eyes meet.

'Good morning,' Imogen nods briefly and rests her arm on her old man's shoulder. 'Zack's running me over to the Whitechapel Gallery. I want to have a look at the Rothkos.'

Outside in the street, a hairy-looking geezer is leaning against a Porsche. He looks what I have always fancied being – working class arty. Getting all the crumpet but being mean, moody and uncouth with it.

'All right, dear.' Crispin pats her hand and she goes out without even a glance in my direction.

'Every business has a few teething troubles,' continues Sid. 'It's probably a good idea to get all the buggers out of your system in one go.'

'Bugs,' I say. Out of the window I watch the way Hairy

Bonce gives Imogen's arse a crafty feel-up as he guides her round the front of his motor. I bet they are going straight round to his pad. How could she do it? I thought that we had something special. Something different.

'But you told me that you were both skilled craftsmen,' whines Crispin. 'I have a reputation to uphold.'

'But we are skilled craftsmen,' says Sid. 'We don't know nothing – I mean, there's nothing we don't know about renovation and all that. It won't take us a moment to get Miss Murdstone's place tidied up.'

'Miss Murdstone has made it clear that she never wants to see either of you again,' says Crispin, grimly. 'Really, I hesitate to give you another assignment.'

'Don't worry, Crispin,' soothes Sid. 'We've been involved in much bigger cock-ups than that, haven't we, Timmo?'

'That's right,' I say. 'That wasn't a typical example of what we can do.'

Crispin groans and runs his fingers through his hair. 'Wallpapering,' he says. 'Can you wallpaper?'

'Well –' I say.

'Of course,' says Sid. 'We can do it on our heads.'

'I'd rather you did it on the walls,' says Crispin. 'I've got a client, small flat, couple of rooms plus mod cons, won't take a jiffy. Only needs one of you.'

'Timothy,' says Sid. 'Just his cup of tea. He'll do a lovely job for you.' Crispin looks at me expectantly. Sid looks at me threateningly.

'What's the address?' I say.

I don't feel like a lot of argy-bargy because I am dead choked about Imogen. Birds have given me the elbow before but they don't usually get in quite so fast after the main feature. It makes me think that my tender, innocent young body was being used. That is the worst of being sensitive. You leave yourself open to exploitation.

Bargrave Villas looks like a Victorian railway station and lives in North London. Parcels of flats are grouped around various staircases and number fifty-one is on the third floor. The bell-push is in the middle of the door and since I have my arms full with rolls of wallpaper and a bucket, I attempt to lean forward and press the bell with my forehead. As I do so, the door opens and I nearly kiss the top of the head of the bird who opens it.

'Oh!' She starts back nervously which is perhaps not surprising.

'I'm sorry,' I say, dropping half a dozen rolls of wall-paper. 'I was trying to press the bell with my nut. I'm from Home Enhancers. Is it all right if I get cracking?'

The bird is slim and has black hair and red eyes. I think she must have been crying. Maybe Miss Murdstone rang up and told her I was coming.

'Oh yes,' she says. 'Yes. I suppose you might as well do it. It'll add to the value of the property, won't it?'

'Definitely!' I say. 'It's a very nice pattern you've chosen.'

'I didn't choose it,' says the bird. 'It was my – my husband. Too bad he's not going to be here to enjoy it!' She looks as if she is about to burst into tears.

Oh dear! Don't say I've put my foot in it, seconds after getting through the door. 'I'm sorry. Is he – er – ?'

The girl nods. 'He's left me. Gone off with another woman.'

'Oh, thank goodness for that,' I say. 'I mean –! I thought he might have been dead.'

'No such luck!' says the bird bitterly.

'Yes,' I say. 'Well – er, I guess I'd better get on with it. I'll try not to disturb you too much.'

The girl looks at me thoughtfully. 'Very well. Let me know if you need any help. The kitchen is at the end of the passage.'

'Ta,' I say. The bird takes another long gander at me and goes into a bedroom.

Normally, I would be interested in any interest she showed but I am still recovering from my experience at the hands – and other things – of Imogen. Even at this moment she is probably – no! I can't bear to think about it. I must bury myself in my work and shut out all thoughts of Hairy-bonce slipping his sizzling sausage into Mrs Fletcher's fun-bun and turning himself into a hot dog with a side order of nature's mustard.

I take a butchers at the two rooms I have got to paper and find to my relief that they have been emulsioned. The paper can go straight on the walls. Into the kitchen and I pour the paste powder into a bucket of warm water. It doesn't half pong nice. Almost like a bird's perfume. The subtle niff wafts round my hooter and I turn to find – blimey! Mrs Richmond has shed her slacks and jersey and is wearing a play suit that looks as if it has been painted on her by a spray gun fitted with telescopic sights. The pong is definitely her own and her face has been brightened up by the addition of some craftily applied make-up. To a man not stretched on the rack of a shattered love affair she would look very fanciable.

'Finding everything all right, are you?' she says.

'No problems so far,' I say.

She hovers before me for a moment and then picks up the Radio Times and willows out of the room. From behind, she looks like a couple of cats in a sack. Percy hoists one of my goolies a couple of millimetres and then goes back into mourning.

I lay some sheets of newspaper along the wall of the lounge and give the paste a stir. It looks like frog's spawn. I have never hung any wallpaper before but I am certain it is very easy. You just press it against the top of the wall and then smooth it out. There are always a few wrinkles but they disappear as the paper dries. I spread the roll out along the kitchen table and bend down to pick up the brush. When I straighten up, the paper has curled up again. I put the brush back, unroll the paper, stand the iron on the end of it and – the paper curls up from the other end.

'All right? Still winning?' By the cringe! Mrs Richmond is now wearing a long black see-through nightie with a big pink bow underneath the tits. What has got into the woman – no help from the audience, please.

'Fine,' I say, wrenching my eyes away from the festival of knocker. 'It won't be long now.'

'You don't find it too warm, in here?'

'It's all right for me,' I say.

'I find it very close.' Mrs Richmond accompanies this remark by brushing against a sensitive part of my anatomy as she replaces her *Radio Times*. 'Nothing on,' she says.

'I beg your pardon?'

'Nothing on the telly,' she says. 'Sometimes they have a film in the afternoons.'

'I know,' I say. 'Anna Neagle. My Mum watches them.'

'Oh.' Once again she glides to the door. 'See you later. If you want everything – I mean, anything, I'll be in the bedroom.'

'Roger,' I say. For a moment, her eyes widen hopefully. 'I mean, I understand,' I say.

What a funny woman. There is something about her manner that suggests I might be able to lob my ferret up her coney hatch without fear of reproach. Still, that is not the kind of thing I am interested in at the moment. Work is my life.

I measure out a strip of wallpaper, cut it, and weight it down on the kitchen table. Now for the paste. I reach for the brush and find that it has slipped below the surface.

Knickers! By the time I get it out, my hands are covered in paste. What a blooming nuisance! The paste has set much thicker than I thought it would and has got more lumps in it than Mum's porridge. This I find when I slap some on the paper. There is clearly more to this wall-papering lark than I had thought. I pick off as many lumps as I can and smear them on the edge of the sink. Now for the big moment. I remove the weights and carefully lean forward and peel the paper off the table. Easy does it, that's it. Fantastic! I was terrified that I might tear the paper and have to start all over again. I carry the paper into the lounge and choose a spot fairly near one of the corners so that I have a vertical line to work with when positioning the paper. I may not have done this before but I am no – oh, Fuxbridge!! I am holding the paper with the sticky side towards me. What a twit!

'Are you all right?' Mrs Richmond is nuzzling my left arm. I must not let on that I am making a pig's arse of everything.

'Lovely, thanks.' I turn my head to give her a confident smile and – eek! She is only wearing a pair of dark blue lace panties. I thought it felt funny when she nudged me.

'How are you going to get it on to the wall?'

Good question, Mrs Richmond. Go to the top of the form and piss off. I concentrate hard, take a deep breast – I mean, breath – you can see the effect the woman is having on me – and try and turn the paper round and pin it against the wall with my elbow. The paper folds like a book snapping shut and the two sticky surfaces are glued firmly together.

'Oh dear,' says Mrs Richmond. 'It's got stuck, hasn't it?'

'Yes!' I shout. 'It's got stuck! Now do you mind very much leaving me alone!?'

Mrs Richmond's Manchesters begin to tremble in time with her lower lip and she turns on her heel and runs from the room. I start to follow her and realise that I have still got the wallpaper stuck to my hands. I try to straighten it out and then give up and crumple it into a sticky ball.

When I get to the kitchen, Mrs Richmond is sitting hunched up at the kitchen table, sobbing her heart out.

'I'm sorry,' I say. 'I didn't mean to be rude.'

'You were right, you were right!' she wails. 'I behaved like a tart. I asked for it. I don't have any confidence in myself any more. I just wanted to prove that I could attract someone – that I'm not a reject!'

Hot tears run down her cheeks and drop on to her knockers. It is very effective stuff and quick to warm Timmy's heart – and regions southwards. Her situation is not so unlike mine – only much more serious, of course. I too have tasted rebuff. How selfish of me to be only thinking of myself when there was a fellow human being in need of sucker – I mean, succour. Suddenly, I forget about Mrs Fletcher and decide to concentrate on my client's problems. Of course, it is not all pure goodness of heart. I have always found that the quickest way for a bird to get to my hampton is through her own tear ducts.

'Careful,' I say. 'You've got paste on your-er, oh well, it doesn't matter – look, you mustn't blame yourself. I know how you feel.' This is not one hundred per cent true but by the time I have slid my sympathetic arms around the lady's trembling shoulders and dropped them down to the soft cave of her belly, then I do begin to get some idea of how she feels.

'You don't have to be sorry for me,' she sniffs.

'I know I don't,' I say.

'You'd better let me go and put some clothes on.'

'I don't want you to go,' I say. I am not lying, either.

'I've made a complete fool of myself.'

'No you haven't.' I kiss away one of her salty tears and

remove a bit of paste from her nipple with the side of my little finger.

'I'm not all that ugly, am I?' she says.

'No, I say. 'Just sort of average.'

'You're making fun of me.'

'That's right.' I bury my head in the angle of her neck and shoulder and gently tug at her flesh with my teeth.

'Are you doing this because you're sorry for me?' she says.

'Yes,' I say.

I move my mouth over hers and spread my fingers across the back of her head. Her hands slowly slide round me and squeeze me tight. As our lips stack, my right hand drops into her lap and starts to interfere with her underclothing. Nothing to get you pulled up in front of the beak for finger smuggling but a soft, rhythmic caress ruckling her panties and rippling over her short and curlies. She starts to say something else but I kiss her silent and quickly slip my hand inside the blue lace. Percy is quivering like a tuning fork activated by a steam hammer and as I send a couple of cuticled hombres riding into love gulch Mrs Richmond presses back against her chair and shoots out her parted legs. Too bad that one of them collides with my paste bucket and sends it spinning across the floor. A thick pool of lumpy gunge surrounds us. Fortunately, my client seems sufficiently preoccupied not to take any notice. Of course, I should clean up the mess right away but – 'Go on! Go on! That's heaven!' Mrs Richmond bites her lip and grips my wrist in a "leave me if you dare" gesture. Percy is now mounting a determined assault on the front of my trousers and it is clear that his thirst for action matches that of my abandoned client. 'Take your clothes off!' she grits.

'I thought you'd never ask,' I say. I stand up and start to take off my tank top. I have just got it off both shoulders when – whoops! I step in the spilt paste and slip backwards. My jacket hooks over one of the kitchen chairs and I am pinioned by own weight, arms at side.

Mrs Richmond looks alarmed for a moment and then smiles. 'You're at my mercy, aren't you?' she says.

I struggle to find a foothold on the floor but the wallpaper paste has made it like ice. I do feel a berk. Mrs Richmond rises slowly to her feet and I can see a lop-sided triangle of minge fringe peeping over her half-lowered panties. She steps forward carefully and grabs hold of the tab of my zip. Percy strains forward like a golden retriever knowing that 'walkies' time has arrived. The tank top is stretched tight between my shoulders and I can't move.

'Going down.' Mrs Richmond pulls down my zipper and percy lunges forward like a grandfather clock under a dust sheet. Mrs Richmond unhooks my pants and my equipment bounces into the vertical. 'You're not going to run away from me, are you?'

I nod my head as my client's fingers lightly scamper the length of my love wand. 'Hickory, dickory, dock, the mice run up the cock,' she coos, gracefully hooking her thumbs into the waistband of her panties and steering them floorwards with an educated wriggle of her hips.

I make another vain attempt to find a foothold. 'Can't you help me up?' I say.

Mrs Richmond straddles my hips and closes a hand around my hampton.' 'Don't worry,' she says. That's exactly what I'm going to do.'

CHAPTER FOUR

In which Timmy does a job for the Slobovian ambassador, General Garstlia, and comes to a wet and sticky end with a beautiful South American lady called Conchita.

'Two weeks!' says Sid. 'Two weeks to do a little wall-papering job? You'll have to do better than that.'

'Hang on a minute,' I say. 'It took two weeks because you kept taking me away to do other jobs. Taking the roof off that place in Enfield, for instance. I'll never know why we had to do that. We were supposed to be building a surround to cover in the bathroom basin weren't we?'

'You do it because it puts the customer in your power,' says Sid. 'Whip off the roof and they won't start complaining for fear you'll abandon them. There's a lot of little wrinkles in this building lark. I'm surprised you haven't noticed them.'

'You mean, like the way we never finish one job before we move on to another one?'

'Exactly,' says Sid. 'You always take on more work than you can do so you can make more money. The art is to flit about a bit so you can have a little nibble here and a little nibble there and not let the punters get too dissatisfied. As long as they see you for about an hour a week they're usually quite happy. You can always say that you've got a bloke off sick or there's a shortage of materials – there usually is a shortage of materials anyway. Spinning the job out is good from the costing point of view, as well. By the time it's finished and way over estimate you can say that all the prices of the raw materials have gone up or you had to use more expensive stuff because they'd run out of the items you'd specified.'

'You seem to have got the hang of it very quickly, Sid,' I say.

'I don't want to boast,' says Sid. 'But I reckon that's my Charlie Forte. Crispin is a very good bloke when it comes to the chat-up but he's a bit naive on business principles.'

'Or the lack of them,' I say.

'Precisely,' says Sid. 'Still, now he's come up with a little goldmine I can't be too hard on him.'

'What is it, Sid?' I say.

'The Slobovian Embassy. I reckon it could be keeping us in custard powder and knickers for the rest of our naturals.'

'Big place, is it?'

Sid leans forward confidentially. 'Revolutions.'

'Is it on wheels?' I say. 'Blimey! I knew the world was going through a tough time but I never thought they'd start moving embassies into caravans.'

'You daft twit!' says Sid. 'I'm talking about punch-up-type revolutions, aren't I? Slobovia is in South America and they have a new government every few months. No sooner will one lot have decided on a decor than they'll be out on their ear and a new lot will move in. It will be like painting the Forth Bridge.'

'Have we got a chance of doing that?' I ask. 'Why don't we give them a special price and get the other three as well?'

'Try and concentrate on one thing at a time,' says Sid. 'I'll provide the mental dynamism. And tart yourself up a bit. We've got to see General Garstlia. You've finished that Richmond job, haven't you?'

Bearing in mind Sid's instructions about not getting to grips with the lady customers I have deemed it inadvisable to tell him the real reason for the job taking two weeks. It is not just lousy workmanship, oh dear me no. That unfortunate lady needed an enormous amount of reassurance that she was still a fanciable property. I was getting about two strips of wallpaper up for every one of the other thing. Another couple of days and thc bags under my eyes would have sunk so low that I would have been able to carry my balls in them. Fortunately, her old man put me out of my misery. I went round there one day and found that he had come back – good job he didn't do it twenty minutes later. I could not help smiling to myself because he was practically on his hands and knees to her. He obviously reckoned that he had been a very naughty boy. Little did he know the chopper-chafing that wifey had been dishing out. The morning he returned was the one I finished one and a quarter rooms in two and a half hours.

'Oh yes, Sid' I say. 'I used my loaf and spun it out a bit like you said. Of course, there are those other little bits of unfinished business we were talking about earlier. . . .'

'Don't worry about them,' says Sid. 'They can hang on a bit longer. I want to put everything we've got into this one because it's going to be Rosie's first job.'

'Rosie's first job?' I say.

'Yeah.' Sid looks slightly uncomfortable. 'She's always had a leaning towards interior decoration.'

A thought both coarse and objectionable springs to my mind but I reject it as being unworthy of me. 'I know,' I say.

'She's done a few things with Crispin but this is going to be her first solo effort. It's a bent she's always wanted to give vent to.'

'You've got to give vent to a bent,' I say. 'It's becoming quite a little family venture, isn't it? Do you think you'll be able to find an opening for Dad?'

'I've had one in mind for some years,' says Sid grimly.

'Down at Wandsworth Cemetry. Dead handy for the nick, so I'll be able to pop in and see you after I've dropped off the flowers. No, but seriously. I'm right behind this idea of working together as a family unit. I think that a return to the ideal of family togetherness is the only hope for the world. I mean, if you can't trust your own kith and kin, who can you trust?'

'What a bleeding depressing thought,' I say, after a moment's consideration. 'Can't you come up with something better than that?'

'Family togetherness is not depressing, you stupid moon-faced git!' snarls Sid. 'If you really think it is I'll punch your teeth down your throat!' Sid has his own quaint way of putting his principles into practice and I decide that a change of subject would be a good idea. 'This General bloke. Who's he when he's at home?' I ask.

'General Garstlia is the Slobovian Ambassador to the UK.' says Sid. 'He's a very important geezer.'

'I should think so,' I say. 'I mean, a general. That's really something, isn't it?'

'Not in Slobovia it isn't,' says Sid. 'They don't have a rank in the army lower than colonel. I believe it's the copper mines that helped his career along.'

Whatever it is, I am quite excited when we roll up outside the Slobovian Embassy in London's fashionable Belgravia. One of the perks of this kind of job is that you get the chance to take a shufti at how the other half live and I have never been exposed to one of the South American variety before. I believe that they are very hot-blooded and passionate – at least that is what I was told by the copy on the back of the last Chili Con Carne packet I looked at.

'All right,' says Sid, his finger poised before the bell push. 'Let's have no cock-ups.'

Rosie sighs and pats her hair. 'Really, Sidney! Must you

be so coarse? You're not cleaning windows now, you know.'

Rosie is wearing a pair of flair bottom slacks and a fun fur that is more of a laugh riot. It niffs so much that I reckon the goat must have been glad to get rid of it. On her bonce she is wearing a turban. Sid does not reckon this at all but I think she is trying to look like Carmen Miranda. Knowing Rosie as I do, he should be grateful that she is not balancing a bunch of grapes and a couple of bananas on top of her nut.

'Hadn't we better wait for Crispin?' I say.

Sid looks at his watch. 'Nope. If he's late, it's too bad. We want to show these geezers we're on the spot on the dot. That's a good slogan that, isn't it? "On the spot on the dot."'

'Yeah. It would be great if we were running a mini cab business,' I say.

Sid pauses with his hand wavering in front of the bell-push. 'That's not a bad idea –'

'Oh, shut up!' says Rosie, shoving Sid aside and pressing the bell firmly. 'Just concentrate on this, will you? If you latch on to my business colleagues you're going to have to see things through.'

Sid is swift to take umbrage at this remark and unpleasantness is only averted by the door being opened. 'Yes please?' The bird has just given the perfect answer to my unspoken question. She is petite, with full, sensuous lips; dark, flashing eyes, swept-back hair and big knockers that really fill out the distance between her shoulders. Down in the hammock of my Y-fronts, percy whispers 'Olé!'. If this is a typical example of Slobovian womanhood then I will book my passage tomorrow – come to think of it, I wouldn't mind booking her package either.

'Home Enhancers,' says Sid in his best "pleased to meet you" voice. 'General Garstlia has granted us the privilege of dancing attendance upon his august personage.'

'You, dancers?' says the bird, sounding puzzled and looking at my bag of tools. 'August? Is July now. Why you come early?'

'We have an appointment with the General,' says Rosie, briskly pushing in front of Sid. 'Try not to make a fool of yourself Sidney.'

'You'd think they'd understand plain English in an embassy, wouldn't you?' grumbles Sid as we are conducted along a corridor. 'It's enough to make you break off trade relations.' So saying, he trips over the outstretched legs of a geezer wearing a sombrero and a blanket who is propped up against the wall like a guy. Immediately, the bloke snatches up a rifle, leaps to his feet and fires a couple of shots into the ceiling. Large quantities of plaster fall on Sid's head and there are shouts of 'I surrender' in several languages – I know about this because I found a piece of paper that Dad kept in case he was called up in the last war. It even had the Italian for 'I surrender', which shows that he was no taking chances.

While we cower against the wall, a door opens and a man wearing a dress uniform and riding boots comes out with his hands above his head. 'It's alla lies about the nuns,' he says. 'Some of my besta friends are nuns.'

This bloke may not be a dead ringer for Richard the Lion-heart but he is no slouch when it comes to summing up a situation. Quick as a flasher he has snatched the gun – no great problem because the geezer's sombrero has fallen over his eyes – and is pointing it at Sid's gut. As a slimming aid it must be unique because Sid's belly changes from convex to concave as I look at it.

'So,' he says, all menacing-like. 'Another revolution thwarted. Let there be dancing in the light well outside the basement window. I will personally supervise the executions.'

He raises his shooter like he intends to air-condition Sid, but the bird who opened the door steps forward swiftly. 'No, Excellency,' she says. 'These are the decorators.'

A disappointed expression leaks across Garstlia's face. 'But I have no more room for decorations,' he says. This is indeed true. Every square inch of his chest is covered in medals and ribbons.

'It is the walls we have come to decorate, Your Excellency,' says Rosie with a shy humility that I have not heard for many a long day.

Garstlia's eyes sparkle and his Zapata moustache lurches ten degrees towards the horizontal. 'Quel grandilente balloonos!' he says gazing at Rosie's knockers. 'I think we maka sure they no carry bugging device.'

Before anyone has woken up to what is happening, he is running his evil hands all over Rosie's mammalian appendages. I must say, she takes it very well – mind you, at the risk of appearing unbrotherly, I must reveal that this is not the first experience of that type she has had to contend with. Mum was very worried about her at one stage. I remember the time when she was at school and Dad caught her on the front room settee with the exchange teacher – I think he was called an exchange teacher because after his appearance at the South Western Magistrates Court he changed to doing something else.

Unfortunately, Sid is less well-equipped to deal with General Garstlia's slightly eccentric behaviour. 'Get your hands off my wife!' he shouts. 'What do you think you're doing?'

'I already tell you what I am doing,' says Garstlia, shoving his hand up Rosie's jumper. 'I check for bugging device, secret weapons, combine harvester – anything that take my fancy.'

Sid moves forward like he is out to deliver a bunch of fives and Garstlia waves his equaliser threateningly. 'Calm yourself, Sidney,' reproaches Rosie. 'The General is only trying to do his job.'

'This is ridiculous!' says Sid. 'He shouldn't have to do that.'

Rosie does not answer but pulls forward the neck of her jumper and addresses the General's head which has now thrust itself up under the tightly stretched wool. 'Are you satisfied, General?'

'He didn't even take his hat off,' complains Sid. The General wriggles into view again and Rosie pulls down her jumper. 'Satisfied?!' he says. 'You think a son of Slobovia is so easily satisfied? I show you how I am satisfied. Macpherson!'

So saying, he sits down on a chair and starts unbottoning his tunic. Seconds later, a bloke wearing a high-peaked cap and jackboots sticks his long snitch round the door. He has a duelling scar on one cheek and is wearing a monocle. He does not look like a typical Scotsman. 'You hev called me, Excellency?'

'Si, Macpherson,' says Garstlia, extending a foot. 'Remova my boots. I am instituting an athletic security check.'

'I notice it's only women you check,' sneers Sid. 'You're not interested in what I might be carrying.'

Garstlia does not say anything but catches Macpherson's eye and nods towards Sid. Macpherson acknowledges the gesture and advances on my brother-in-law. A swift upward movement of the knee and Sid is lying on his back clutching his groin. 'Dida your educated knee reveal anything?' says Garstlia.

Macpherson shakes his head. 'There is nothing there,' he says.

'I'm grateful for a second opinion,' says Rosie, dropping to her knees beside her stricken husband. 'Can we stop all this searching and get on with some work?'

'I don't think that bloke is a Scotsman,' I say. 'He looks more like a German to me.'

'Gott in Himmill Hempstead!' snaps Macpherson. 'Vot a dirty lie! "Tis a braw bracht moonlit nacht, the noo!" Hogmannay, Haggis, Harry Lauder and "Lang may your lum reek"! Heil Hitler!'

'I'm sorry,' I say.

'You don'ta know what you are talking about, Englishman,' says Garstlia. 'Otto Macpherson was a ghillie in the Bavarian Alps before he –'

'Scottish Highlands!' hisses Macpherson.

'– Before he came to Slobovia in nineteen forty-five with his fiend Martin Boor –'

'My friend has nothing to do with it!' screams Macpherson. 'I come because I love wild life. Can we Scots never be allowed to forget?'

Further discussion on the problems of ex-patriot Scots is interrupted by the arrival of Crispin Fletcher, looking harrassed. 'I say, I'm most awfully sorry to be late,' he says. 'I fell asleep at the sauna. I don't know who – I mean, what came over me.'

'Thank goodness you're here,' says Rosie. 'I'm afraid Sidney hasn't been handling things very well in your absence.'

At the moment, Sidney is handling his goolies with something approaching tenderness and it is only with the greatest difficulty and the support of the rest of us that he regains a vertical position. Whether his hampton may ever do the same is a matter for conjecture.

'Excellent,' says Crispin, nervously rubbing his hands together. 'Now let's get down to work. Rose, you come with me. Our two technical tiros can embrace the mechanical nitty gritty.'

In practice, this means getting the air-locks out of the central heating system. We try bleeding a few radiators but this does not work so Sid suggests draining the whole system and refilling it with the taps open. When the water starts coming out we will know that all the air-locks have been cleared and will close the taps. Dead simple, isn't it? How fortunate I am to have a partner with Sid's easy grasp of matters technical.

While the unpleasantness has been going in the hallway, it has not escaped my attention that the Slobovian bird has been hardly able to take her eyes off me. At first, I think my fly must be undone but as time passes it becomes clear that my animal magnetism is at work. When I smile at her, she blushes and peers down over her knockers like she wonders if she will ever see her belly button again. When it is time for me to go round and visit the radiators she is swift to offer her services as a guide.

'Do you like working here?' I ask as we go into a box-room at the top of the stairs.

To my surprise – Conchita – that's her moniker. Nice, isn't it? – puts her fingers to her lips and advances towards me until her cakehole is practically brushing against my ear. 'You must be careful,' she whispers. 'General Garstlia is a great bugger.'

This news comes as something of a surprise to me. On his track record with Rosie, Big G has looked normal plus. Still, you can never tell these days. More and more people are trying to be all round entertainers. Maybe it is just an old Slobovian custom.

'Thanks for the tip,' I say. 'It's not my bag of walnuts, I don't mind telling you.'

'Sssh!' Conchita taps a vase of flowers that for some

reason is standing on the window sill. 'Little bug.'

'It's a greenfly,' I say. 'They don't do any harm – not unless you're a leaf.'

'Ssssh!!' Conchita lifts the flowers and pulls out a small microphone on the end of a lead. She does something to it and drops it back in the vase. 'Now we can speak,' she says in a normal voice.

Of course, the minute she does that, I realise what she was on about. What a twit I am! Especially after what Garstlia said he was doing to Rosie when he was trying to find the switch on her knockers.

'I'm sorry,' I say. 'How stupid –'

Conchita holds up a hand. 'You must not apologise. You are not used to such deviousness. Oh, how I wish my life could be free from taint.'

'You are in publishing?' I ask.

'No, it is Garstlia. He is a man of no principle and less integrity. He is not a gentleman like you.'

'Gentleman?' I say.

'You are English, no?'

'Yes,' I says. 'But –'

'Always, I have longing to meet with Englishman. So cool, so refined. Lacking the coarse, passionate fibre of my countrymen. As a little girl, I love Biggles.'

'I've never tried one,' I say. I suppose it must be some kind of muffin or suchlike. It is funny how these foreigners always have tastes for local delicacies you have never heard of. I remember an Arab geezer who was always on about Gentlemen's Relish. For a long time, I thought he was talking about a J Arthur.

'And your sense of humour,' she says. 'So dry, so sophisticated.'

'It's nothing,' I say. 'Nothing at all really.'

Of course, one never thinks that a foreign bird could find

a British bloke romantic, does one? I suppose it's just the same for them as it is for us. What the eye doesn't see, the imagination reckons must be a bit of all right.

'It is important for me to take a grip on myself. I become easily excitable – uncontrollable almost. You would despise me.'

The bird is actually quivering as she stands before me. I stretch out a hand to take her arm and she flinches. 'You'll find me very understanding, my dear,' I say, trying to summon up my recall of how George Sanders used to come over.

'All the time that I have been here I have hoped to make the acquaintance of an Englishman but I am never allowed to leave the embassy. It is like a prison.'

'How too, too trying for you,' I say. 'So I'm the first British chappie you've been able to feed your peepers on?'

'Please?' she says.

I squeeze the hand that now nestles between mine. 'I imagine that in your own country, men must never cease from telling you how beautiful you are?'

Conchita sighs and flutters her long eyelashes at me. 'Never in words. It is always the grab and the pinch. The General he is typical Slobovian. Uncouth, like animal. He has never heard of croquet pitch.'

'Poor devil!' I say, gently transferring my hand to Conchita's upper arm and stroking downwards in what I hope is a soothing and reassuring gesture. 'There are moments, of course, when passion dictates the conduct of the heart.'

'How beautiful you speak,' she says. 'I wish that I could match you with the words.'

'It is not necessary,' I say. 'You are the violin, I am the bow. I will play you with my lips and we will make beautiful music.'

Not bad, is it? I bet that if you were an impressionable Slobovian bint you would feel yourself going at the knees. The trouble is that you can't talk to a British bird like that or she would think you were barmy.

Conchita closes both mince pies and strains as if trying to break an invisible bond. 'Be still my foolish heart,' she says. 'There are other radiators to be visited.'

She makes a feeble attempt to remove her hand from mine but I cling on to it like the double-six in a domino shuffle. 'Don't move,' I say. 'This moment may never return again. We are but grains of sand on the beach of time. Our days are numbered like those flowers – incidentally, why are these flowers in the boxroom?'

'There are flowers in every room,' says Conchita. 'When the Russians get a new bugging device they give us the old one. At the moment, we are being flooded with plastic flowers.'

'*Plastic* flowers?' I say. 'If those flowers are plastic, why is there a greenfly on them?'

'It's probably an American spy,' says Conchita. 'You would be amazed at some of the devices being used in the cold war.'

'Cold?' I say. 'How can lips so warm utter such a word?'

'This is madness,' breathes the Slobovian bombshell. 'Your words incinerate me. I am a volcano about to erupt.'

'Lava come back to me,' I say, cursing that the bird will not be able to understand my little joke. 'Don't feel ashamed. Your impulse to rip all my clothes off and make violent love to me is thoroughly natural. You could be certified for doing anything else.'

'You mean, you would not spurn me?'

'You did say "spurn", didn't you?' I say, after a pause. 'Yes, I can guarantee that I won't spurn you.' With these reassuring words, I draw the fortunate bird into my arms and give her a tongue sandwich with a side order of rampant banana served through a bulging trouser leg. I have heard expressions like "releasing the flood gates" but I have never had an experience that measures up to the description – until now.

The moment we start necking, the bird presses herself against me so tightly that I think she is trying to force her tits under her armpits. She grinds her cakehole against mine and makes growling noises like it is feeding time at the lion house.

In the circumstances, it seems cruel not to open the presents until Christmas Day so I pull down my fly and taking Conchita by the wrist, guide percy to the promised hand. The pressure on my north and south eases as she suddenly sucks in her breath. Her fingers hesitate and then close like those of someone about to start a motor bike. Before she can deliver any revs, I slip my right hand underneath her skirt and start to gently caress the inside of her thighs. Despite all her rabbit about having a passionate nature I do not reckon that she is a survivor of a lot of bouts of in and out – if any – and I do not want to alarm her. A hand up your bird is not always worth two on her bush – not in the long run, anyway.

For those of you who are saying hang on a minute! I thought this bird was supposed to go a bundle on refinement, let me elucidate you – it's all right, it won't stunt your growth. If Garstlia had done what I have just done, it would have been crude and nasty. It is all in the mind, see? Birds are like that. If one geezer shoves his mit up their bloomers then he is a pestering little nit or a sex maniac. If Mr Right does it, then he is demonstrating what a firm, positive, no-holds-barred, red-blooded and desirable male he is.

Conchita clearly slots me into the second category.

'Caramba!' she breathes. 'Que hombre! When you do that it is like the hot sun on the Andes.'

'You keep your Andes to yourself,' I say, revealing that even at moments of advancing passion I am not above leavening the conversation with a small geographical joke.

'What you say?'

What I really feel like saying is 'Where are we going to do it?' The boxroom of the Slobovian Embassy shows no sign of being equipped with a four poster bed and things are getting to the point where – 'AAAAAAAARRRRRGGGG!!' 'Que grandos cojhones!'

'Thank you.'

While Conchita continues to juggle with my goolies I cast an eye round the room. There is something on top of that cupboard. Could it be? Yes! An old, dust-covered Lilo. No doubt used for sun-bathing on the embassy roof.

'Hold on a minute.' Conchita does as she is told and I gently have to remove her sensation-hungry fingers. I wonder if she plays the marraccas, as well? I shake the Lilo and prepare to inflate. Should the results be anything like those already achieved by percy then I might have a small airship on my hands. 'I make love bed,' I say by way of explanation.

Conchita nods approvingly. 'May I take clothes off?'

'As you wish,' I say, trying to retain my cool. I might as well invest the occasion with all the finesse the lady so clearly requires. I take a deep lungful of air and start to blow. Thank goodness, the lilo does not seem to have any leaks.

Before me, Conchita is down to a skimpy bra and panties. Coffee coloured, they are, with tiny white polka dots. She hesitates for a moment and then reaches behind her back. Blimey! When she takes off her bra, I nearly cop back all the air I have put into the lilo. What a cracking pair! The nipples alone are like the sockets of a couple of screw-in light bulbs. And that cleavage! If she lay on her back you could use her as a bike rack. 'Multo splendido!' I say giving her a few of the fruits of my cosmopolitan upbringing. 'Multos bigos!'

'You no find them vulgar? I think they too large for English lady.'

'English lady not going to get them,' I say through gritted Teds. Never at a loss for a romantic gesture, I remove my cakehole from the lilo and apply it to one of the afore-mentioned strawberries (Strawberry ripple: Nipple. Ed.). Hardly have I changed the switch from blow to suck than Conchita shivers like a bamboo shithouse in a typhoon and hurls herself into my arms. It is obvious that the knocker-nibble looms large in her legend. You have heard of 'See Naples and die'? Well, this is more like 'Seize nipples and cry'. Unfortunately, I am still holding the lilo in front of me and the force of her passionate embrace half deflates the perishing thing up one of my nostrils. If you ever feel like blowing your brains out, I suggest you find another way. This method might get the kink out of General Amin's hair but that is about all.

'Forgive my clumsiness,' begs the trembling curve carnival. 'It was because I had to kiss you. I cannot control myself. When you touch me, I get pimples.'

'I think you mean goose pimples,' I say firmly. 'I have every sympathy with your feelings but please try and keep them under wraps until I get this thing blown up. Your restraint will enhance the satisfaction of both of us.' With these cautionary words, I start blasting air into the lilo like I intend to sail over the North Pole under it. Conchita watches me like I am demonstrating a rare skill and plucks impatiently at my shirt. If I can't make this chick then I might as well jack the whole thing in and take up flower arranging.

'Would it disturb the delicate balance of your feelings if I removed your trousers?' She does put things nicely, doesn't she?

'Just ease them down to ankle level,' I say.

Still clinging to the lilo I blow until I am dizzy and feel for the nozzle plug. Knickers! There isn't one. Conchita's pants are turning into groans. If I don't get a move on she could start without me. The nearest thing to me that will fill the hole is the radiator plug. There is still no sign of any water coming out so it won't make any difference if I borrow it for a few minutes. I can soon replace it when something starts happening. A few deft screws from the dexterous digits and the lilo is sealed. Wacko the froggies! Let the full frontal assault on the furburger commence. I chuck the lilo on the floor and slide my arms round the one hundred and fifty per cent willing Conchita. She has carried out my instructions to the french letter and my trousers are nestling coyly round my ankles. With practised skill I ease myself out of my shoes and kick myself free of the lingering embrace of the wool/terylene mixture. Now there are only two pairs of pants worn like fabric hoops to separate us. As our lips clamber over each other, our fingers ease the unwanted underclothes floorwards.

'What should I do now?' says Conchita.

'I think if you lie down that will be a move in the right direction,' I say, trying to stop the drool exploding down my chin.

Nine chicks out of ten you suggested this to, would lie on their backs and not risk ruckling their knockers, but my new friend hits the lilo on her tummy and shows me one of the most beautifully shaped pairs of back bumpers that it has ever been my mince pies' pleasure to roller coaster over. She turns her head and flashes those dark brown eyes at me and percy lunges forward like a dragster quivering on the starting line. There must be a bit of the old jungle magic inside me because the sight of that chick makes me grit my Teds and revert to your friendly neighbour moggy deciding that there is a lot more to life than pissing over the catsmint.

I drop to my knees so fast that I bounce off the lilo before nuzzling my way between Conchita's thighs. As her legs flop open, I slide my hands under her thighs and tilt her body forward so that her rave cave is poised temptingly before my hampton. Her hand reaches behind her imploringly but before it has reached the small of her back, I have potted my red and brought two other balls up within a centimetre of the pocket.

'OOOOOOOOOOH!!' sobs Conchita. 'Is good!'

I have no reason to disagree with the lady and proceed to slide percy to and fro until it feels as if he is running on buttered silk. If I had half as easy an action with a cue I would be world snooker champion, no trouble. While the mighty wurlitzer is pounding out love's sweet melody, my greedy hands shake forward and give Conchita's top bollocks a friendly fondle. If you want to develop your wrists, vicar, this is the sport for you. Her breast works settle into the palm of the mit like a couple of cannon balls.

'Turn over,' I say. 'I want to look at you.' This is not the whole truth. I want to save my wrists for the next pint I have to lift, and also, I prefer to get to the front door by coming straight up the drive. I don't like to go round the side of the house.

Conchita turns over fast – almost too fast – and her perfect white Teds smile up at me. 'Is this how you do it in England?' she asks.

'I do it the same anywhere,' I say. 'Mostly like this but with a few other things thrown in for variety.'

'Things like what?' she says.

'Things like this,' I say, lowering my voice a couple of octaves and my head a few inches. It is just a common or garden love dive – very common, and better in the garden because there are usually fewer people about – but Conchita goes spare. Her back arches like a sheet being shaken in a gale and she thrusts forward so that my epiglotis is practically having it away with her clitoris. She says a lot of funny things in Spanish that I don't reply to and starts to wrench out handfuls of my barnet. This is all very well but if she tugs me any closer she is going to suffocate me.

'Gerrofflefluvme!' I say – it is not easy to speak with a mouth full of furburger. I jerk my head free and launch myself forward until I am in the perfect position to despatch my thigh-snitch into her snatch.

'Come!' Like a shoplifter whipping a can of baked beans into her bag while the store detective's back is turned she takes my tonk up to the belly button – I can practically feel my bum touching the small of my back. 'Fug me! Fug me!' She hollers.

Her English may be faulty but the sentiment she is expressing is universal. It is amazing how many upper class birds – and Conchita must be upper class if she works in an embassy – like to talk dirty in the sack. It turns them on to shout a few naughty words. It also goes down a treat if you whisper a few horrible sentences into their lugholes. You see you have to face up to the fact that your really upper class bird is slumming when she offers you the freedom of her crutch-hutch. It isn't your mind she is interested in. The least you can do is give her her money's worth. Tell her you are going to shove your unmentionable up her unspeakable and a happy flush of pleasure will richochet through her fundaments faster than a dose of clap through a monastery.

'OOOOOOOOOOOOOH!!!' When Conchita grabs hold

of your arse, you realise why it has a cleft in the middle. You have to put up a fight to withdraw far enough to get a good swipe at the target. Wham! Wham! Wham! Percy drives the message home and I hear the healthy 'thwack' of my circulars banging against the tradesmen's entrance.

'WAAAAAARRRRRRGGGGGGHHHHHH!!!!' Conchita's love yodel drowns the puny sound of my bouncing balls like the Atlantic Ocean slopping into a teacup and she grabs me like I am the last life jacket on a shipwrecked liner. I have know some tenacious birds in my time but this chick makes a limpet seem like a phantom weight bantam weight. Suddenly I find that I have no control over what is happening. I am in the remorseless grip of a flesh machine, seemingly engaged on a ruthless programme of self destruction. My rudder shudders as I judder up and down on top of the Slobovian flesh fortress and the air is pumped from my body as surely as it was from the crushed lilo.

'No!' I gasp. 'No!!'

Conchita does not seem to be interested in my problem – eg survival. 'I like,' she says. 'You tickle my fancy.'

'Tickle it?!' I say. 'I'm practically double-glazing it.'

'I no understand,' gasps Conchita. 'You tell me again when we finish foreplay.'

Foreplay?! Who does this girl think she is? Or, more important, perhaps: who does she think I am? Half an hour later, I am no wiser regarding the answer to either question. All I am, is knackered. What that girl has done to me should not happen to the french letter used by the Highland Light Infantry. I lie back gasping for breath and the ceiling revolves above me.

'That was lovely,' I hear a voice saying that sounds like mine.

'What you mean, was?' says Conchita.

'Well,' I say. 'Er-it was-you know-um-I've got a job to do, haven't I? – somehow.'

To my amazement, Conchita burst into tears. 'I knew this would happen,' she sobs. 'I have offended you, haven't I? My passionate nature has unbalanced your delicate susceptibilities. You no longer wish to continue with our love-making.'

'It's not so much a question of wishing –' I begin.

'All my life I dream of this moment – and when it comes, I destroy it. I think I kill myself!'

'No!' I say. 'You mustn't do that. The business couldn't stand it – I mean, your sweet young life is too important to be thrown away over anything so trivial.'

'But if you no longer desire me –'

'I do desire you,' I say, signing percy's death warrant with four words and my sympathetic nature. 'Of course, I do.'

Fifteen minutes later – give or take a couple of heart attacks and a dizzy spell – I pass out. At least, I have no other explanation of how the time is filled until I open my eyes and hear a strange gurgling noise. At first I think it must be Conchita and me drifting apart – I appear to be lying on top of the lady – but a turn of the head reveals an astonishing sight. As my mince pies glance off the slumbering bonce of Conchita they are swift to locate the source of the noise. It is caused by the water that is beginning to rise above that escaping from the deplugged radiator. Your reaction to those words may well be as was mine to the actual situation – amazement coupled with a slowly dawning comprehension. The room is two and a half foot deep in water and the lilo is floating on top of it. Conchita and I must have fallen asleep about the time Sid started refilling the hot water system. Oh my Gawd! What am I going to do? I suppose I could start bailing the water out of the window but that would take about three days even if I had a bucket. The one thing that must not happen is for someone to open the door. That would be –'

'Inna here, Mrs Chompley. Nobody willa looka for us in here.'

'Oh, General Garstlia. You are a one!'

'No!' The last voice is mine and coincides with the door-knob turning. Like a puff ball sucked away by a mountain torrent, Conchita, the lilo and myself are swept down the marble staircase as General Garstlia and a beturbanned Mrs Chompley are knocked sideways by the backwash. I catch a glimpse of a Hoover vacuum cleaner turning a lazy circle in the air and then the ornate ceiling gives way to a vista of grey sky. Somebody must have opened the front door. Oh no! As we sail through and swoosh down the steps I can just imagine how annoyed Sid is going to be.

CHAPTER FIVE

In which Timmy samples the pleasures of the water bed with Miss Finch and suffers cruelly at the hands of a devilish German invention.

'Belgravia!' says Mum. 'Oooh that's not very nice, is it?'

'It *is* very nice,' says Sid. 'That's the trouble.'

'That's what I meant,' says Mum. 'Oh, Timmy. You do know how to make me unhappy, don't you?'

'I suppose if it had happened outside Battersea Town Hall it would have been all right,' says Dad. 'That's what you make it sound like. I find the whole episode repulsive and disgusting. I don't care where it happened.'

'I'm sorry, Dad,' I say. 'It won't happen again.'

'I should bleeding hope not!' says Sid. 'The law of averages must see to that. You can't end up stranded in the middle of Belgrave Square on a lilo with a naked tart more than once in your life, can you?'

'Sidney!' says Mum. 'Language!'

'What do you mean, language?!' shouts Dad. 'It's not often that I have to agree with sponging git-face here but his anger seems to me well-founded. It's Little Lord Fauntleroy who's the source of the family's iggy-inno-inog –'

'Ignomy,' says Sid.

'When I want your help, I'll ask for it, you berk!' says Dad pleasantly. 'Until then, belt up! What I'm trying to say is that I've had enough of your accessories, my lad. I'm fed up with turning the other cheek. Parents today have too many laxatives, that's the whole trouble with this once great country of ours. When I came back from the war –'

'Hang on a minute,' says Sid. 'What war are you talking about? I know you stand up and salute every time the bus goes past the Cenotaph –'

'He doesn't do that any more since he flattened his Homburg,' says Mum.

'I wish he'd flatten his humbug as well,' says Sid. 'We all know Dad's war record: Vera Lynn singing "The White Cliffs of Dover".'

While Dad goes to some pains to explain that the Fire Watchers did as much to win World War II as the blokes who waded ashore on the Normandy Beaches, I take the chance to go and lock myself in the karsi. One advantage of having a family who are as punchy as ours is that they can never dwell on one spot of aggro for more than five minutes without another totally different outbreak flaring up. In this permanent smokescreen of unpleasantness it is easy for the original offender to creep away

I think that the incident at the Slobovian Embassy marks the beginning of a deepening rift between Sid and Crispin. When I ask Sid what Crispin has lined up for us, he gives a bitter laugh and says 'a firing squad'. Certainly, we don't get any new jobs from that quarter and Sid is reduced to advertising our talents in *The South London Sentinel* and a couple of tobacconists' windows. Not an easy task, I might add. Frankly, I couldn't see anything wrong with 'We do big and small jobs all over your house'. Still, there is no accounting for the way some editors' minds work, I suppose. In the end we have to settle for 'Worried about your plumbing? Can't get it up? Home Enhancers will have a go at anything. Satisfaction guaranteed'.

'That should do it,' says Sid. 'We don't want to be too pacific. Cast the net as wide as possible. We might find ourselves getting work we never thought of when we started out.'

In this last respect Sid is proved right beyond his wildest dreams. My first call is to South Chelsea – or Battersea as it used to be known when I was a little lad. It is a nice flat with a view overlooking the park – completely overlooking it, in fact – and a handsome brass door knocker. No sooner have I delivered a sharp rat-tat-tat than the brass knocker disappears and is replaced by a couple of handsome fresh numbers doing battle with the front of a too-tight fluffy wool sweater.

'Good morning,' I say, addressing the bristols and wrenching my eyes in a northerly direction. 'Home Enhancers at your service.'

'Come right in, darling.' The bird's tone is about as breezy as February in Great Yarmouth and she moves to onc side like I am a bull rhino at the end of a one hundred and fifty yard run-up. 'What have you got in your dear little bag?'

'Tools,' I say.

'How lovely! Can I have a look?' The bird is small with short, black hair, sharp features and bright, shining eyes that open wide to emphasise her words.

'Er – yes, I suppose so,' I say. Nobody has ever asked to look at my tools before.

The bird, who is apparently a Miss Finch, drops to one knee and pulls open the neck of my bag. I can't help noticing that her brown velvet trousers are stretched so tight that you could not get a starving bus ticket between them and the tempting curve of her back bumpers. VPL (Visible Pant Line) is in evidence and percy twitches like a cat dreaming of fat mice.

'I say! This one looks rather groovy. What is it? Some kind of manual vibrator?'

'That's a brace and bit,' I say.

'I've never used one,' says the bird. 'You'd need long arms, wouldn't you?' I don't quite know how to answer this question but it doesn't matter because Miss Finch has tenderly replaced the brace and bit and withdrawn a screw driver. 'This reminds me,' she says. 'Could you have a look at my Multi-Thrust Maxi-Probe while you're here? I think there's a faulty connection.' She straightens up, gives a little shiver and pouts her lips at me.

'I don't think I've ever handled one of those,' I say. 'Do you still have the instructions?'

Miss Finch shakes her head and her boobs wobble temptingly. 'I threw them away. They were in German, anyway.'

'They make a very good article, the Germans,' I say, trying to sound as if I know what I'm talking about. 'Very good on the electrical side, they are.'

'You can say that again, darling,' says Miss Finch enthusiastically. 'Would you like a drink before we get down to it?'

'Well, a cup of tea would be very nice,' I say.

'A cup of tea?! How freaky. I'm sorry but I can't gratify you. We don't stock it. Scotch? Gin?'

'Maybe later,' I say. 'When I've finished. Apart from the Maxi-whatsit, what did you want me to do?'

To my surprise, Miss Finch takes me by the hand and leads me into a bedroom. 'Amaze me by your versatility,' she says.

I am not quite certain what she means so I take a butchers round the room. I imagine I am supposed to suss out what needs doing. The bed is certainly in need of attention. It is flopping all over the place and looks more like a thick polythene mattress. 'I'll start with the bed,' I say.

'Traditionalist, huh? I like that. Tea and bed. I should have laid on a crumpet for you.' What a funny lady! You do meet some strange people in this kind of job. I haven't really been on this bird's wavelength since I came through the door.

'Let's get your electrical problem out of the way,' I say. 'I have to warn you that if it's complicated I won't touch it. I don't want to give you a shock, do I?'

'Just a little one might be rather heavenly,' murmurs Miss Finch. 'Anyway, I'll leave it to you. After all –' she squeezes my arm into a new shape '– you're the expert.'

Whilst I am pondering on the reason for this gesture, the bird rises on tiptoe and gets something down from the top of the wardrobe. At first I think it a miniature cannon or seige gun. It's long nozzle rears upwards at an angle of forty-five degrees from a horizontal platform and there is a length of electric flex running away from the firing mechanism. I am about to express the kind of reaction I usually reserve for my nephew Jason Noggett's headless model soldiers – Jason executes each one of his toys, seconds after it comes into his possession – when I notice something familiar about the shape of the cannon's barrel. Something very familiar, not to say downright rude. It has a bulbous, swelling head with a cleft on the lower side and a-hang on a minute! I know that artillery pieces recoil after they have been fired, but they don't slide backwards and forwards in the manner that Miss Finch is demonstrating.

'This is what the little goody is supposed to deliver,' she says, wistfully. 'Do you think you can fix it?'

I don't say anything for a few seconds because it is slowly dawning on me what this little masterpiece of Teutonic technology is all about. It is a mechanical dildo – or artificial dick as it might be more generally known. You obviously sit astride the platform, position yourself accordingly, press the switch and – oooh! It is almost too naughty to think about. A few more of those down at the Conservative Club and percy would be on half time. It just goes to show that the Krauts don't only think about rockets and dirty great sausages all the time – I don't know though. Maybe that is why they turned out this little number. Their big V2 base was at Penismuncher or somewhere like that, wasn't it?

'Um,' I say. 'I haven't seen one – er quite like this before. What makes you think I can do anything with it?'

'Your ad., darling. Reading between the lines, it's easy to see the service you really provide – or should I say sevices?' Before I can properly digest her drift, the saucy little minx has started to whip her woolly over her nut. Could it be that there has been some misunderstanding about the nature of the activities undertaken by Home Enhancers? I had better put the record straight immediately. After all the trouble there has been lately, it would be too bad if . . . cor!! What a lovely pair of Manchesters! The minute they start doing an Ali Shuffle in front of me I begin to reconsider my position-in fact, quite a few positions. I don't want to give offence, do I? If there has been something misleading about our advertisement, the onus must be on us to put things right.

'It may be a loose connection,' I say as her flushed features emerge from the other end of the sweater. 'I'll just pop out and get my screw driver.' Light moves at one hundred and eighty thousand feet per second. I think I may be a fraction slower as I duplicate the distance to my hold-all. As her eyes widen in appreciative surprise I whip off the motor housing and see that my original surmise was correct. One of the connections has come adrift.

'Is it going to be difficult?' she says.

'Uh-hum,' I say thoughtfully. 'I think the retarded

manifold may have sheared off against the percussion booster.'

'That's amazing,' she says. 'You can tell all that by just looking at it?'

'It's only a gift,' I say. 'Honed to a fine edge by years of experience' – I got that from a razor ad on the telly.

'Is it going to be possible to fix it?' The look of pleading confidence is something to behold – in fact, I have never seen a girl who looked so pleading confident before.

'It should go back to the factory,' I say, shaking my head glumly. 'Still –' her face lightens a fraction in anticipation of an arrest of the galloping gloom – 'if I can bridge the gap between the jump switch and the input-output socket, I may be able to do something.'

'You're wonderful,' she says. 'Really wonderful. Do you know that?'

'I've heard rumours,' I say modestly. 'Keep your fingers crossed and I'll see if a chance in a million is going to pay off.' I make the connection, place the contraption on the bed, and press the switch. Immediately, the artificial hampton starts to glide smoothly back and forth.

'Poetry in motion!' breathes Miss Finch, popping open the front of her fly. 'Come to your mummy, my dinky doo!' She twists a knob and the deadly doughnut-duffer speeds up its action to a rate I would find hard to imitate without battering my balls into discs.

'Ah hem,' I say. 'Now, about this bed –'

'You'll find it heaven once you get the hang of it,' says Miss Finch enthusiastically. 'It's super for everything – even sleeping.' So saying, she wriggles out of her velvet trousers and peels off her panties revealing a cute little furry grotto situated where you would be disturbed to find a tattoo of a tiger with its mouth open. 'Hurry up,' she says. 'Otherwise I might decide to make do with Uncle Fritz.'

She lies down on the bed and positions herself so that her drawn-up thighs are on either side of the rampant robot.

'Hang on!' I say. I can't take this standing up, can I? The whole world may have gone gadget-mad but there are some things that are still best left to traditional methods. Like somebody has shouted 'Blast Off!' I shred my threads and dive on to the bed. This is where I get another surprise. The bed is like nothing else I have ever been on. It ripples beneath me and clings to every contour of my body. As I stretch out towards the delectable Miss Finch, she seems to shimmer beneath my hand.

'It's heaven, isn't it?' she murmurs. 'These water beds are fantastic. With one of these and the Multi-Thrust Maxi-Probe at my fingertips, I find that the knob of the television set accumulates dust.'

One of the few knobs within grabbing distance that has a chance to, I think to myself, as Miss Finch's doughty digits collide with my dongler. I give her the benefit of my mouth and send my hand down to explore her nether lips. One of the surprising things I find with ladies is that experience seems to be unrelated to size. You would think that Miss Finch had seen more Mad Micks than your fat Uncle Arthur has had hot dinners but her ouch-pouch is small and neat as a mouse's earhole.

The water bed is indeed a new sensation and while I scout round the head of the valley, I get used to the way that it ripples with every motion of my body. Miss Finch's hand sinks deep between my legs and she runs her forefinger slowly to the head of my action man kit lightly dusting the inside of my thighs with her other fingers. It is not the stuff to make you think of enrolling as a Trappist monk and percy lunges forward twice as eager for action as a fasted ferret. Miss Finch grabs the root of many of my problems and it is clear from her determined efforts to drag the rest of me after it that she is desirous of intercourse. I am not slow to accept the hint and as I rocket into her socket, the miracle of German craftsmanship topples slowly to the floor. From its irritated whirr it seems unhappy about missing out on the action but I am not in the mood to extend sympathy. The only thing I am extending is percy who seems to be responding as if Miss Finch's snatch has some magic growth ingredient. Four hundred gallons of water swish about underneath us and it is necessary for me to slide my protective mits beneath my client's back bollocks in order to ensure that we don't suffer the same fate as the Magni-whatsit. Once you get used to the challenge, it is something more than pleasant and I sense that my efforts are serving to bring satisfaction to the lady. Little things tell me this – like the way she tries to bite through my jugular vein or her determined attempts to sharpen her finger nails on my backside.

All through this simple unaffected jollity the only bar to my total enjoyment is the noise made by the teutonic tonk. They don't give up in a hurry, the krauts, you know. The Multi-Thrust Maxi-Probe probably works under water – not of course, that there would be a large demand for its services under such conditions. Still, with chicks like Miss Finch about, you never know. Now that I have become used to the particular challenges posed by the water bed, it might be a good idea if I tried to silence 'Uncle Fritz'. Rising to my knees, I lean over the edge of the bed and see that the Maxi-Probe is expending its energies against the bulging polythene. Poor old Maxi-Probe. It looks rather pathetic, really. Especially, now that the knob has dropped off and there is just that metal screw scraping against the side of the – hang on a minute! Before I can take any protective measures, Miss Finch yanks me down on top of her again.

'Don't stop!' she pants. 'I'm coming! OOOOAAAA-RRRRGGGGHHH!!!'

I may have left out a few Hs and Gs but that is roughly what it sounds like. 'Don't!' I say. 'Stop it! We're in terrible danger!' I don't know if you have ever tried to reason with a woman in a situation like this, but you are wasting your time, take my word for it. Once they get carried away they go faster than a used french letter tossed over the side of Niagara. Of course, I should indulge in a spot of coypu interrupted but you know me, I am so weak. Once I hear the mating call of the Great Crested Furburger I am off like a greyhound from a burning trap. 'YYYYYAAAAAHH-OOOOOOOOOOOOO –'

My happy yodel is interrupted by a noise like someone ripping apart a piece of muslin and the bed disappears beneath me. For a fraction of a second, Miss Finch and I are pressed against the floorboards and then the backwash from both walls tosses us into the air like a couple of puff balls. The treacherous Maxi-Probe has got its revenge for World War II.

'Oh no!!' squeals Miss Finch. 'What are we going to do?'

'Don't worry,' I say. 'I've got a cycle repair kit in my hold-all.'

CHAPTER SIX

In which Timmy gets to grips with Mrs Butler's plumbing and manifests symptoms of a strange and terrifying complaint.

Unfortunately, the cycle repair outfit is no good. It does not seem to cater for two foot long rips. I suppose they find it difficult to get that length of patch in one of those little tins. Miss Finch is most upset, especially when the Maxi-Probe fuses and disintegrates in a shower of beautifully turned, kraut nuts and bolts. I think it is the best thing that could have happened because it can't be good for her to become addicted to a thing like that, can it? I try and point this out but she tells me to piss off – not in so few words but that is the gist of what she is saying. Even when I suggest that we clamber on to the settee for a spot of muff planing she is not interested. Women are so changeable, aren't they? I suppose the fact that half the other people in the flats are banging on the front door does not help very much. The doors do not have the nice, tight closure they had in the Slobovian Embassy – all the better for sound proofing and picking up pieces of indiscreet chat on the bugging devices, you see – and the caretaker in the basement cops so much water that he has to dive into the flood to rescue his budgie from drowning. In the end, I decide that the only thing to do is present my bill and scarper. At least, I mended her dildo before it blew up. Would you believe that the ungrateful gretchen refuses to cough up and even threatens to sue me under the Trade Descriptions Act? Marvellous, isn't it? You sweat your balls off for people and what do you get? Two sweaty balls stuck in the top of your socks. I am so disgusted that I leave without collecting my tools. It is only when they hit the pavement in front of me as I step through the front door that I remember. I am dead choked because the bubble in my spirit level is never the same again and my adjustable spanner won't adjust.

I am worried that Sid will look unfavourably upon my efforts to satisfy Miss Finch but when I limp back to Clapham's answer to Paul Newman it is to find him with other things on his mind besides a couple of inches of thinning barnet. 'I think we may have to change that advertisement,' he says, shaking his head.

'Funny you should say that,' I say.

'I was hardly through the front door when this bloke asked me to test his block and tackle,' continues Sid. 'I thought it was a bit strange when he asked me to slip on the manacles!'

'One would,' I say.

'Still, he seemed a nice enough bloke. Mind you, I wouldn't have gone horseriding in a pink velvet leotard.'

'How do you know he'd been riding?' I ask.

'He had this riding crop in his hand,' says Sid.

'Of course,' I say. 'Sorry I interrupted. What happened next?'

'Well, it was a bit funny really. No sooner had the manacles snapped over my wrists than he hauled me into the air so that my toes were just touching the ground.'

'So the block and tackle was working?'

'That's what I told him. "Strap me –!" I said. And, do you know what happened?'

'I've no idea, Sid.'

'Before I could say anything else, he shipped my overalls

down to my ankles and started laying into me with the riding crop!'

'That's terrible, Sid,' I say. 'What did you do?'

'I didn't do anything,' says Sid. 'I mean, it's not easy with your hands manacled above your head. Use your common.'

'But you must have tried to reason with him?'

'He wasn't very hot on the reasoning. I think the only thing he said was "Whoah, my proud beauty!" '

'So how did you get out?'

'I kicked him down the stairs of the crypt. I swung back on the pulley and lashed out with both my feet. Caught him smack in the bread basket. Then I managed to hook a chair towards me and –'

'The crypt?' I say, 'They only have those in churches, don't they?'

'That's right,' says Sid. 'Didn't I tell you? This geezer was a fire escape.'

'Didn't you think it was a bit strange?' I say. 'A vicar wearing a pink velvet leotard and carrying a riding crop?'

'I thought he was one of those sporting parsons you read about,' says Sid. 'I'm always prepared to think the best of people until they prove me wrong.'

The long and short of it is that we change the advertisement: 'Sidney and Timothy bend over backwards to give you satisfaction. Nothing is too big or too small for us. Our tools are at your command'. We don't have any more trouble after that.

Where I do have a problem is in the area of bed. After the unhappy incidents at the Slobovian Embassy and Miss Finch's place I can hardly bring myself to lie down on one. The minute I get in a horizontal position, feelings of queasiness and nausea flow over me. It is just like when you are really pissed.

And when I do drop off, I have the most terrible dreams: being washed down the side of one of the pyramids on a bath mat, being passed out of an enormous pipe hundreds of feet above the sea – only it is not really a pipe as I see when I hit the water – some of the stuff I come up with makes a Ken Russell movie seem like the childhood of Julie Andrews. If it is like this when I am on my tod, what is it going to be like with a bird? Will I ever be able to tangle with a hampton throttler again?

The lady who supplies the answer to this question is called Mrs Butler. The minute she opens the front door a voice inside me says 'hello, hello!' She has passed the high peak of her loveliness but is clearly in no hurry to teeter down the other side. There are lines round her eyes but they are well concealed and although she pats her hair nervously, hardly a wisp is out of place.

'Oh,' she says. 'You've caught me unprepared. I didn't think you were coming until tomorrow. My husband will be here, then. He knows all about it.'

He would need to, I think to myself, taking in the lady's well-stacked frame. She is built like a settee that is just getting to the comfortable stage and you could eat your breakfast off her knockers.

'Oh,' I say. 'I'm sorry. Do you want me to come back?' Mrs Butler rests a hand on her bristols and studies me with some care. 'Er-no,' she says. 'I think it will be all right. I can show you what the problem is. It's rather a messy job I'm afraid. Are you conversant with blocked up sinks?'

I am not quite certain what she is on about but it does not pay to shake your head in this game so I flash my Teds and follow her into the kitchen. Very nice, it is. Real dentist's waiting room magazine stuff. I cast an eye over the sink and it is indeed blocked. 'You've tried caustic soda, have you?' I ask.

'Oh yes. I tried that and some other stuff. Didn't do any good.' Mrs Butler gives me another searching look. 'If I can leave you to get on with it? I've got one or two . . .'

'Of course,' I say. I much prefer it when they piss off. The more they stand around looking over my shoulder, the more inclined I am to make a cock-up. I get underneath the sink and undo the nut on the S bend. Water pisses down on to the floor and it occurs to me that it would have been a good idea to arm myself with the washing up basin before I started. At least I have proved that the blockage is not between the sink and the first bend which is quite good going for me. Now comes the difficult part. I mop up with a handy tea towel and consider what to do next. While I am in full ponder, a haunting wiff assails my hooter. It certainly does not come from the drain so I order my nut to do a sharp right turn and find myself trading eyeballs with the lovely Mrs Butler. She has not slipped into a see-through black negligee plunging down as if late for an appointment with her belly button but it is obvious that she has been tarting herself up. Her lips sparkle in the thin afternoon sunshine and there is a fresh fall of powder over her upper cheek bones. Above all, and speaking a language more powerful than even that found written on the walls of the karsi at the Notting Hill International Friendship Club is her perfume. Phew! – or, if you prefer it – Cor! This stuff does not take many prisoners I don't mind telling you. A few whiffs of that and the elastic in your Y-fronts starts to come out in a rash of five o'clock shadow.

'How's it going?' says the lady.

'I'm just getting to grips with it,' I say, absent-mindedly wiping my hands on one of the kitchen curtains. I see the direction in which Mrs Butler's eyes are travelling and stop hurriedly. 'Sorry about that,' I say.

'Don't worry,' says Mrs B. 'I was going to change them

anyway. I'll leave you to it, then. Give me a shout if you need anything.' She gives me a little smile and pats her hair again. 'It would be so much easier if Frank was here. It's a nuisance him having to go to Birmingham.'

'Er – yes,' I say, wondering if they can niff her on the outskirts of that fair city. 'Well, I'd better get on with it, hadn't I?'

'Yes.' Mrs Butler looks as if she is going to say something else and then purrs off like a well-sprung scent tanker. I have been in this kind of situation before and it seems not totally beyond the realms of possibility that Mrs B is flashing out the odd mating call: the tart-up, the scent, the reference to hubby being sixty miles away. Normally, this information would cause a friesian of interest to pass through my action man kit but today I feel nervous – yes, nervous. I know that if I get on a bed with that woman, the ceiling will collapse or a tidal wave burst out of one of the cupboards. I go dizzy just thinking about it.

The best thing to do is to stick to the job in hand. I shake my head to clear the last wiff of niff out of my hooter and start tracing my way along the pipe after it leaves the S bend. It comes out of the kitchen fitting and runs parallel to the wall for six feet before disappearing through it. Just before the final bend is a nut which clearly holds two pieces of pipe together and it occurs to me that if I disconnect the pipe here and rod it back to the S bend I may be able to clear any gunge that has built up in the horizontal stretch. Fascinating, isn't it? No? Oh well, you obviously don't have a mechanical bent. People used to feel like that about Leonardo da Vinci.

I get my adjustable spanner – my new adjustable spanner – and start to try and loosen the nut. By the cringe, but it is tough! I pull out all the clamps that hold the pipe to the wall before I begin to shift it. Finally, as the plaster rains down like the first warnings of an avalanche, it shears clean off and the severed pipe gobs up a fast widening pool of disgusting black liquid. Bollocks! Just what I didn't need. Now I will have to find one of those machines that puts a thread on piping. Still, I mustn't get discouraged. I will finish the job and come back to the pipe later.

I find another tea towel and do some more mopping up. Ugh! This black stuff doesn't half niff. The contrast with Mrs Butler's love pong is enough to make a Rangoon refuse collector heave up all over his loin cloth. A glance at the tea towel suggests that its useful days are over so I bury it in the waste bin under a layer of potato peelings. What the eye doesn't see . . . I am now ready for the rodding. The only problem is that I don't have any rods. Fortunately, the initiative of a Lea is second only to that of Napoleon Bonnyparts and my eagle eye is swift to seize upon the possibilities offered by one of the brass curtain rails above the sink. That will do a treat. It is a pity that I leave a few potato peelings and a spot of gunge on the curtains as I take them down but you can't make an omelette without breaking eggs. Still, I had better try and clean myself up a bit. I turn on the tap and hold my hands under it before I realise that the waste pipe is still disconnected at the S bend. Silly Timothy! The water splashes off my boots and starts to dilute the remains of the black muck that is smeared all over the kitchen floor. Honestly! It turns you right off, doesn't it? For no fault of your own everything suddenly starts to foul itself up. Still, this is where the real calibre of a bloke shows itself. Time for a spot of true British phlegm and mucus. The old bulldog spirit that for centuries has – oh, knickers! I have got muck all over the cuffs of my new crocus-pattern, slim-fit, French styled, poplin shirt. I knew I should never have worn it for work.

I carefully put the curtains somewhere where it is only

rank bad luck that allows them to drop into the pool of gunge and pick up the curtain rod. From the thickness of the muck that has leaked out of the pipe it seems quite likely that this is the reason for the blockage. A few deft strokes of the rod and I will have more than earned the embarrassingly large fee which Sid charges for what he calls 'Lightning' jobs. The slight difficulty that I have, concerns the problem of finding enough room to manoeuvre the rod before shoving it up the pipe. In the end, I have to bend the pipe away from the wall which leads to a further fall of plaster and a fresh pool of gunge. With some little difficulty, I manoeuvre the curtain rod so that it is wavering above the refrigerator and – oh dear, just my luck! It has to flick an electric mixer on to the floor, doesn't it? I never knew they had so many attachments – I suppose they are attachments? It certainly is a pity about the eggs. Difficult to know how many there were now that so many yolks are broken.

'Oh!' If I was suddenly struck deaf, my hooter would tell me that Mrs Butler was standing behind me. 'Having trouble, are we?'

'Nothing serious,' I say. 'It's going very smoothly on the whole. I'll have this lot cleared up in a jiffy.'

Mrs Butler stands in the doorway, her foot hovering above the ground while she tries to find a clean piece of lino to put it on. 'I was going to suggest a cup of tea,' she says, looking at the kettle as if across a minefield.

'I'll pop the kettle on,' I say. 'By the time it's boiled I'll have the problem sorted out.'

Mrs Butler looks as if she is not totally convinced and delivers herself of a deep sigh. 'I hope you're right,' she says.

'Have trust in Home Enhancers,' I say. 'We won't let you down.'

'Y-e-e-s.' She hovers for a minute and then pushes off. Now for it! Grandstand finish. I plug in the electric kettle and ram the rod up the pipe a few times. You would not think that a little lead pipe could carry so much muck. It's fantastic, it really is. I have definitely located the root of the problem. Just to be on the safe side, I put a plastic bowl under the end of the pipe and turn on the tap. Quite a lot of the water that bounces back off the refrigerator goes into it. It is a pity about the rest of the water, but at least it shows how well I have unblocked the pipe. Sid would be proud of me if he was here. Now I had better connect the two pieces of pipe. I don't have time to find the machine that puts the thread on pipes so I will have to use my initiative again. I know! If I cut the finger off one of the washing up gloves and snip off the end, that will make the perfect link – look out Einstein, here I come! Of course, it won't do a lot for the washing up gloves but you can't worry about a few snipers when there is a war to be won. I have seen enough movies on the telly to know all about that. I find a ball of string in one of the drawers – amazing how dirty your hands can get when you do a job like this – and lash the rubber tube to the two ends of pipe. My word! If only this dear old country of ours could show as much initiative, we would not be in the mess we are now.

Now, for the moment of truth. I refit the S bend, turn the tap and – bravo! The escaping water leapfrogs the join, no trouble. I trim the pieces of string that hold the rubber link and stand back waiting for the Queen's Award To Industry. Well done, Lea. Britain salutes you.

Some might be prepared to rest on their laurels but not me. The job will not be completed to my satisfaction until I have cleaned up. The mark of a real craftsman is that he leaves a place exactly as he finds it. CRACK!! There is an unpleasant shattering noise and cracks run across one of the window panes. The steam from the electric kettle has been playing directly on to it. Knickers! Just when I was getting on top of everything, too. I wonder if it has done any permanent damage to the glass. I extend a finger to give a gentle prod and – CRASH! Half the pane shatters on the concrete outside the window. I suppose I had better do something about that. I will get on to it the minute I have put the curtains back.

Of course, what I had not reckoned on was that the inside of the brass curtain rail would become filled with gunge. I give the outside a quick swoosh under the tap but it is not until I am standing in the sink that I notice the black stuff pouring out and running down the wall – well, not all down the wall. Quite a lot of it is absorbed by the curtains. Maybe I should have put them on after I got the rail up. It is so bloody complicated, isn't it? And how they got covered in potato peelings I will never know. Perhaps I had better clean up the floor and come back to the curtains later. The main thing is – keep your pecker up or Nil Desperate Dandum as the poet put it.

In practice, this turns out to be a lot more difficult than I had anticipated. You would never cocoa how bleeding useless the vacuum cleaner is. It doesn't pick up a single broken egg – just scrambles them into the slime. Honestly, sometimes I wonder what hope there is for the country. You seem to be doing it all by yourself, don't you? All this stuff about dust, fluff and grit and the snivelling machine can't even pick up a teeny, weeny yolk. It looks as if I will have to do the whole job with a dustpan and brush. Wake up, England! You're living on borrowed time.

'Oh!!' The daintily enunciated exclamation springs from the glistening lips of Mrs Butler who has slid up behind me niffing as if she has shot a whole flask of love pong down the front of her bodice. 'What are you doing?!'

It is a stupid question because it must be obvious what I am doing. 'Just tidying up,' I say. 'It won't take a jiffy. The kettle's boiled.'

'But the room's a shambles! Look at the curtains – and the window! You've broken the window!'

'That wasn't me,' I say. 'That was the kettle. They can be very dangerous if they don't have a shut-off device. Maybe I could fit –'

'No!' Mrs Butler almost shrieks the word before she regains control. 'I don't think you need do anything else.' Her eye travels along the waste pipe and stops when it comes to the join.

'I've fixed it,' I say allowing a note of modest pride to enter my voice.

'Is that safe?' says Mrs Butler incredulously.

'Perfectly,' I say. 'Watch.' I turn the tap sharply to the right and we both stare expectantly at the slim rubber tube. Maybe, our combined attention is too much for it. The link shivers, then swells up like a balloon. The end furthest away from the sink becomes unattached and a stream of water sprays all over the kitchen accompanied by a very, very rude noise.

'Turn the tap off!' screeches Mrs Butler.

'I'm sorry,' I say. 'Have you got any stronger string? I think the tube is all right.'

Mrs B picks up one of her washing up gloves and counts the fingers. 'Is this what you used?' she says.

'That's right,' I say. 'You can deduct the cost of a new pair from our bill.'

'Bill?' Mrs Butler gazes slowly round her kitchen. I must say, it is looking a bit the worse for wear.

'Don't worry about this lot,' I say. 'I'll soon have it under control. Maybe, if I used a bit of flex –'

'I think you've done enough for one day,' says Mrs

Butler firmly. 'Why don't you go and wash your hands? I'll tidy up in here.'

'I couldn't let you do that,' I say. 'That's *my* job. Once I get stuck into something, I'm a little demon.'

'Ye-es.' Mrs Butler looks at me with renewed interest and sucks in her breath. 'There must be something you're good at. Like a young, untamed stallion.'

'I beg your pardon?' I say. What is she on about? I don't even like horses. That picture Aunt Edna has above the gas fire turns me right off. Six foot white manes blowing in the wind and nostrils like ice cream cornets. No thank you! I would rather have that eastern-looking bird by Tetchy-cough.

'Crude, clumsy strength,' continues Mrs B, breathing heavily. I hope she is all right. She is looking at the vacuum cleaner in a very funny way and running her hand up and down the curved handle. Maybe it would be a good idea if I left her alone for a few minutes.

'I'll pop into the bathroom,' I say. 'I could do with a-a-wash my hands.' She is still looking at me in a very funny way as I go out. Perhaps she has taken umbrage about the mess. It is difficult to tell with women, sometimes.

The bathroom is very refined with lots of little plastic shepherdesses holding soap and bunches of artificial flowers. I wouldn't reckon that it would be exactly the thing that Burt Reynolds would choose but it is very nice in its way. My hands are dirty up to the elbow so I peel off my shirt and jacket and strip to the waist, just like an American movie star who is about to clean his teeth. I have a tart up and wipe myself dry on one of the thick white bath towels – well, it starts off being white. It is amazing how towels attract dirt, isn't it? There is a shelf beside the mirror and on it a bottle of men's cologne called 'GRRRH!!' Bloody stupid name, of course, but I can never resist having a quick slosh under the armpits. If you don't like the niff it can't be worse than what is there already. I have just removed the curiously shaped stopper when Mrs Butler comes through the door – no question of knocking or anything like that.

'No!' she says.

I feel myself blushing as I replace the bottle.' I was just looking at it,' I say defensively.

'That's Frank's,' she says, her features contracting into an expression of distaste.

'I know,' I say. 'I wasn't –'

'I don't want you to smell like him. I want you to be you!'

'Don't worry,' I say. 'I am.'

To my surprise, Mrs Butler puts her arms round me and presses her face to my bare chest. 'Man!' she husks. 'Dirty, earthy man!'

Oh dear! It is clear that my earlier fears were more than justified. The lady is clearly seeking to find my bodkin in the centre of her pin cushion. Normally, I would be more than willing to oblige but the memory of recent disasters is too much with me. 'What does your husband do?' I ask, eager to remind her of her responsibilities.

'Not very much,' says Mrs B.

I wish I hadn't opened my mouth. I can see why Mrs Butler is carrying on the way she is.

'Come upstairs.' Mrs Butler lets out a passionate sigh and her lips tremble against my chest like butterfly's wings. I look down at the ripe swelling of her breasts and imagine them sinking bedward beneath me – immediately I feel sick.

'I'm sorry,' I say. 'I can't.'

'You can't?' Mrs Butler's voice travels upwards at an angle of eighty-five degrees. 'You mean, you've never . . .' Her voice trails away in what I hope is disbelief.

'I promised my mother,' I say. 'Not before I'm married.'

'But that's ridiculous!' says my employer. 'It's 1975, you know.'

'Is it?' I say, looking at my watch. 'Blimey, I'd better be going. I've –'

Mrs Butler has no difficulty in arresting my puny attempt at escape. 'It's not right,' she says. 'A big, strong boy like you. In fact, it's unhealthy. Don't you have wet dreams?'

'Not just dreams,' I say, trying to shut out the picture of thousands of gallons of water washing over me. 'I'm very confused.'

'It shows in your work,' muses Mrs Butler. 'I think I have an obligation to try and straighten you out.' Her fingers move down to the front of my jeans and percy is her first success in the straightening out programme. If we can do it standing up, I may be all right. Best to get out of the bathroom though. The presence of all that water is not good for me. I should never have got involved in the plumbing side in the first place. Once again, I allowed my natural flare to be manipulated. It is like when Sid wanted me to be a lorry driver. I should have put my foot down immediately rather than on the accelerator pedal.

'It's a nice place you have here,' I say, looking round the bathroom.

'It's a nice place you have *here*,' murmurs my new friend, giving percy a friendly squeeze. My, but she is forward. Especially at the front. Evel Knievel would be pushed to jump the gap between her knockers. Talk about Death Valley. If your parachute didn't open you would be a gonner.

'Ah hem,' I say. 'I think I'd better put my shirt on.'

'Don't.' Mrs Butler lays a restraining hand on my wrist. 'If you've got it, flaunt it. Your body has been forged by honest labour. Display it like a standard.'

'You mean, the *Evening Standard*?' I say. 'It would be better if I had a few tattoos, wouldn't it?'

Mrs Butler takes my hand and leads me towards the door. 'Come, my noble savage,' she breathes. 'I will introduce you to the beautiful mysteries of the bedchamber.'

Panic invades me again. 'Couldn't we do it in the passage?' I say. 'We don't want to mess everything up, do we?'

Mrs Butler shakes her head and pats my wrist. 'You poor boy,' she says. 'What strange impressions you must have formed about the sexual act.'

'Wouldn't it be nice, standing up?' I ask.

'It would be nicer lying down in a lovely, snuggy beddy byes,' says Mrs B, throwing open the door of what turns out to be a large pink bedroom. She draws me inside and runs her hand over the bulging front of my jeans. 'I know that he would like to come and lie down with me.'

'He probably would,' I say. 'But he's not the only part of me to be considered.'

'Don't be so silly,' says Mrs B, unpopping her blouse buttons. 'Take your clothes off and swallow your scruples.'

'I'm not double-jointed,' I say, backing against the wall. 'I couldn't even suck my big toe when I was a kid.'

Mrs Butler treats herself to another large breath and expels it in the form of a sigh. 'It's funny how you can be so mistaken about people,' she says. 'I thought you were some shambling, incoherent brute. A man whose rough, horny hands would despoil any woman they came into contact with. A savage, hairy beast wallowing in the deepest pits of depravity.'

'You're probably thinking of my partner, Sidney Noggett,' I say. 'He can get a bit worked up sometimes. There was a terrible scene round at the dry cleaners when –'

'Kiss me!' Before I can tell the good lady about how Sid

refused to leave the shop until they found the button off his blazer, she has chucked herself at my cakehole and is planing the back of my gut against the embossed wallpaper. She has shed her blouse and the fabric of her stretch bra lunges forward appealingly. Uhm. I think I may be able to cope with this lot. Trying to imagine that I am doing it for the first time, I slide my hand up the back of Mrs Butler's skirt. There are a few ruckles of flesh at the top of her thighs and then lovely, smooth fife. She must be wearing some very silky knicks.

Mrs B removes her north and south from mine and rests it against my cheek. 'Naughty boy,' she purrs. 'Is it the first time you've touched a lady?' I nod and wait for the thunderbolt to strike me down. Fortunately, nothing happens. 'It's better round the front,' advises my new friend.

'I am round the front,' I say.

'With your *hand* round the front,' says Mrs Butler patiently. Just to make it easier for me, she grabs my German and places it firmly on top of her furburger. She might be taking a fingerprint. 'Pussy loves being stroked,' she says.

Trying to make it obvious that this is the first time I have strode to the crease, I fumble around like a drunken toddler trying to open its money box in a pair of boxing gloves. As it turns out, this is not the best thing that I could have done. 'I'll make it easier for you, nature boy,' says my new friend taking a step backwards. 'Clothes are so silly, aren't they?'

With these words, she reaches behind her and undoes the catch of her bra – at least, that is what I imagine she does. She may be tapping the Polish national anthem on the small of her back in morse code or seeing if she can work up enough momentum with her elbows to take to the air, but

I don't think so. The fact that her enormous bristols bound forward like released elk hounds and that her bra comes away in her hand supports my contention.

'Do you like them?' she says.

There is nothing she can do about it if I say no, so I nod weakly and watch her toss the bra lightly over her shoulder. I have the feeling that this lady is a frustrated stripper and she is not slow to prove me right. Shaking her nut so that a fresh wave of perfume breaks over me, she takes her skirt zipper between finger and thumb and slowly jerks it floorwards. I bet she would never do that in front of her old man. She needs a complete stranger in order to get it out of her system. I would be very happy to get it into her system but I am still worried about that bed. I know that I would come over all funny if I measured her length on it. The zip won't go any lower and she has unhooked her skirt. Fixing me with an eye like a welk pin, she begins to do a slow shimmy so that the skirt zig zags down her body and ends up in a puddle at her feet. I don't know much about art but I know what I like. Give me a choice between this bird and Toulouse Lautrec and Shorty would have to find someone else to wash out his brushes.

'You like it, don't you?' Mrs Butler is looking me straight in the Y-fronts and percy is making no effort to conceal his whereabouts.

'Come here,' I grunt.

'No, you come *here*,' says Mrs Butler, beckoning me to her all coy-like. 'I've got a lovely present for you.' She sits down on the edge of the bed and begins to tease down her tights. What is the matter with me?! The moment the bed springs start to move, a wave of nausea sweeps over me – it is like turning on 'Stars On Sunday' by mistake. Normally I would leave a trail of scorched pile behind me as I closed the distance between me and that bed but now I cower back against the wall trying not to think of Mrs Butler in the horizontal.

'Come on, dear. There's nothing wrong with you. Take those nasty old clothes off.'

Almost in a dream, I unzip my jeans and flip down my Y-fronts – I used to worry about Y-fronts because I thought they over-heated your hampton. Then I thought about another place where your cream seam gets a lot more crowded and I stopped worrying.

'That's lovely, dear. What are you worrying about?'

Mrs Butler hooks her fingers over the edge of her nicks and thrusts them down a couple of inviting inches. I notice the thin pink lines left by the elastic on her rich, creamy flesh and try and imagine that I am pinned to the wall by steel staples.

'I can only do it when I'm standing,' I gulp.

'But you are standing, dear,' says Mrs Butler encouragingly. 'And very nicely, too.'

'I meant, on my feet,' I say. 'Standing up.'

'You're a funny boy,' says Mrs Butler, softly. 'Funny but rather sweet. Not at all what I thought you were at first.' An expression of some intensity arrives on her face. 'Come here and I'll turn you into a tiger.'

'I don't know,' I say. 'I think, maybe –'

'Come here!' Mrs Butler pushes her panties over her knees and shakes them down to floor level. By the cringe, but she is a comely bit of crumpet! I like them when they are a bit over the top. She must be a regular treasure house of memories and no mistake. Before I know what I am doing I have taken the first dangerous step towards the bed. Foolish Timothy! Mrs Butler lies back against the counterpane and grabs my Mad Mick like she is going to pull a pint with it.

'You know what to do now, don't you?' she purrs.

If only she hadn't lain down. 'I don't think I can,' I say. 'You see, it's all to do with my mother.'

'Your mother?!' Mrs Butler looks alarmed. I can imagine what is going through her mind.

'Yes,' I say. 'It runs in the family. We're all like it. My mother particularly. She's never done it.'

'But what about you?' says Mrs Butler, propping herself up against one of the pillows.

'I've never done it, either,' I say.

'I meant, how could you be conceived if your mother was a virgin?'

'They used an artificial fertiliser,' I say, amazed at how quickly my mind works in emergencies. 'Please don't ask me any more questions, I find it too painful.'

Mrs Butler makes 'tut, tut' noises. 'That's terrible,' she says. 'It must have been a terrible strain on your father – I mean, your mother's husband. Did he make the donation?'

'I don't think Dad's ever made a donation,' I say truthfully.

Mrs Butler closes her eyes. 'You're right. It is too painful to talk about. But –' she slides a hand up the back of my thigh '– you mustn't fear being visited by the problems of your parents.'

'They very seldom visit us,' I say. 'Both Mum's lot are dead and there's a bit of a mystery about my grandad –'

'I didn't mean your grandparents,' says Mrs Butler in a voice trembling with emotion. 'I was referring to your right to lead a normal, healthy sex life – well, not too normal. We don't want to be thoroughly boring about it. Come and lie down beside me and I'll show you what I mean.' One of her hands grabs mine and the other returns to Rampant Reginald.

'It's very kind of you,' I say. 'But . . .' How can I tell her the truth? I can't after what I have already said. The very thought of lying on that bed makes my stomach heave.

'Come here! You don't know what you're missing!'

'Please –!' Before you can say Roger Carpenter, the spilling cornucopia of curves yanks me on to the bed and starts to scramble on top of me. 'No!' I say. 'No! You mustn't!' It is such a change to hear myself saying that.

'Stop struggling!' orders Mrs Butler. 'You'll love it once we get started.'

But we never do get started. The moment my shoulders hit the counterpane, a black, swirling wave of nausea engulfs me. I close my eyes but it is even worse. If I don't get off the bed I will throw up.

'I'm going to be sick!' I shout. Mrs Butler stops trying to pocket my sprocket and watches open-mouthed as I vault from the bed and snatch up my clothes. 'I'm sorry,' I say. 'It's just that . . .' I can't think of anything to say. Mrs Butler bursts into a flood of frustrated tears and I mumble something and go out onto the landing to get dressed. My problem is now a serious one, there is no doubt about it.

Fully-clothed, I go downstairs and stick my head round the kitchen door. Mrs Butler has not done a lot of clearing up. Maybe, I should – no, on second thoughts, I won't. There are some days when it is a good idea to quit before you get too far behind. I collect my tools, wipe my hands on one of the curtains – all the tea towels are too dirty – and open the front door.

Coming up the path towards me is a balding bloke of about forty, carrying an overnight bag and wearing a grey light-weight suit and a harrassed expression. Mr Butler, as I live and breathe faster. What a stroke of luck that I decided to leave when I did. Behind me, Mrs B is still wailing her heart out and I see hubby's already suspicious face becoming more thoughtful. I do hope he is not going to leap to any unfounded and unpleasant conclusions.

'Morning!' I say, cheerfully clanking my bag at him – it is about four o'clock in the afternoon. 'Plumber.'

He is still looking after me as I imperceptibly lengthen my stride and glide speedily round the corner.

CHAPTER SEVEN

In which Timmy seeks medical advice and takes off in the company of Doctor Grimdyke and an attractive sexual surrogate called Judy.

'Doctor Parminter will see you now.'

She is a nice-looking bird. Trim, well-groomed, refined – or maybe it is the white coat. I always feel a bit put down by receptionists. Anyway, what does it matter? She is a woman, and what good are they to me? Unless she likes it standing up, I might as well forget about it. I put down my copy of *Scottish Field* for September, nineteen fifty three – not that the date makes any difference. The contents are exactly the same one decade to the other except for the house prices – and follow the slim, wand-like body of Doctor Parminter's receptionist through the door marked 'Patients seen by appointment only. No smoking. Please do not tear articles from the magazines which are placed there for the enjoyment of otters'. I think it means 'others' not 'otters' but you never know. The way the country is going, the National Health Service may have been forced to amalgamate with The People's Dispensary for Sick Animals.

At first glance, it is difficult to make out Doctor Parminter because he is obscured by a dense haze of tobacco smoke. Then I see this figure with a stethoscope round its neck and specs on the end of its hooter scratching away at a pad. After a heavy bout of coughing, Doctor P taps the specs up to the bridge of his snoz and looks me up and down suspiciously.

'You look strong as a horse,' he says, accusingly. 'Want a few days off work, do you? That's not the way we're going to get the country back on it's feet, is it?' Before I can answer, he starts coughing again. The way he is carrying on, I reckon he is going to snuff it before I have described my symptoms.

'It's not like that at all,' I say, eventually. 'I have a problem I want to discuss with you.'

'You're not on my panel, are you?' No matter which way he looks at you, you get the feeling that he doesn't like you. No wonder he was easier to see than the other six blokes.

'Er – no,' I say. 'The truth is that what I want to talk to you about is a bit personal.' That is why I have come to a new bloke, isn't it? I don't want my local quack grabbing an earful of my little problem. Now that we have Doctor Savumba it has become a matter of national pride. I bet he can get it up in any position, smooth Indian creep! Even Mum says what lovely eyes he has.

'There are clinics that deal with that kind of thing, you know,' says Doctor Parminter looking at me distastefully. 'You don't even need a letter from me. Still, now you're here, I suppose I'd better take a look at you. Stand up and lower your trousers.'

'It's nothing like that!' I have yelped out the words even before Doctor Parminter's hands have closed round the rubber gloves.

A look of fresh irritation rather than disappointment passes across Parminter's face. 'What is it, then?!'

'Well,' I say, looking round and lowering my voice. 'It's to do with my relations.'

'There's no need to whisper,' snaps Parminter. 'The surgery isn't bugged by Barbara Castle. Not yet, anyway. Now, what's all this about your relations? Are they on the panel?' He reaches for a card index system.

'Sexual relations,' I say, feeling my cheeks burn.

Parminter pushes the box away angrily. 'What is it? Premature ejaculation? Right. Here's what you do: wait a few minutes, have a glass of milk, and try again.' I wish he would lower his voice. They must be able to hear him in Balham High Street.

'It's not that,' I say. 'It's –'

'Impotent? Can't gain entrance in the first place?'

'I've only tried the first place,' I say. 'I thought you weren't –'

'Two glasses of milk and some iron pills. Don't wait for the pills to dissolve because they won't. Try and think about something to take your mind off what you're trying to do. A healthy outdoor sport that you enjoy. Mountain climbing, trekking, hiking, hacking –' He collapses into another spasm of heavy coughing.

'It's not the physical side, so much,' I say. 'My problem is more in the mind. I can't have relations when I am lying down. I come over dizzy.'

'That's your wife, I suppose?' says Doctor P, reaching for a biro. 'Dizzy, short for Desirée.' He talks to himself as he writes. 'Patient ashamed to admit that he experiences premature ejaculation with wife, Desirée. Rationalises failure by attributing it to fact that he practises sexual intercourse using missionary position.' Parminter lays aside his pen, takes off his specs, and leans towards me. 'How does your wife feel about this?'

'I'm not married,' I say.

'Not married?!' Parminter leaps to his feet as if stung by a hornet. 'You swagger in here blathering about your sexual inadequacies and you're not even married! You libertine! How dare you vent your impertinence on me?!'

'I'm sorry,' I say. 'I didn't know you had to be married.'

'You have to be married with me!' snarls Parminter. 'Get

out of my surgery, you disgusting little animal!' He rises unsteadily to his feet and then collapses in another fit of coughing. I open my mouth to say something and then decide against it. What is the use? It won't get me anywhere. Parminter's unsteady hand closes round one of the many jars of pills that litter his desk and he is shovelling half a dozen down his throat as I go out of the door. Stupid old twit! For two pins, I would report him to the BMA if I knew what it was.

'Mr Lea?' The bird in the white coat has appeared at my side. 'I'm sorry about that. If I'd known the nature of your problem I'd never have let you see Doctor Parminter. He's rather reactionary, I'm afraid.'

'And bloody old-fashioned, as well,' I say, still stung by the quack's unhelpful attitude. 'I don't know how they dare put up conscription charges. I've never been a strain on the National Health Service and the one time I ask for a bit of assistance I get told to pi-push off.'

'I know,' says the bird soothingly. 'It is a shame. Fortunately, all the doctors in the practice aren't like Doctor Parminter. Some of the younger ones are far more liberated in their attitude to the treatment of sexual problems.'

'That's good news,' I say. 'Perhaps you can wheel me in front of one of them?'

The bird guides me towards the waiting room. 'You'll have to wait a few minutes. If you'll just sit down and read a magazine –'

'I've read that one,' I say. 'It's all about how the red squirrels are being duffed up by the grey squirrels. That, and how a nuclear power station was closed down until a robin had finished nesting in the boiler man's bowler hat.'

'Only a few moments,' says the bird, with a warm smile. 'You'll be seeing Doctor Grimdyke.'

I start reading about the sex life of the red deer and

wonder what Doctor Grimdyke is going to be like. The name does not inspire confidence. Large, cold hands; smelly tweeds, whisky breath, a bedside manner like a regimental policeman in the Highland Light Infantry – I can see it all.

A red light flashes, a buzzer sounds, and the lady in white is standing beside me again. 'This way please.' I follow the bird down a corridor and she smiles at me encouragingly.

'You'll find Doctor Grimdyke quite different to Doctor Parminter.'

Never was a truer word spoken. Doctor Parminter was not a bird for one thing. When I go through the door, I think that I must be in another waiting room. It is so comfortable. Settees, floppy chairs, a shaggy carpet – all very light and airy. The slim, sophisticated bird sitting behind the low table, puts down her copy of Forum and rises as I come in. 'Thank you, Judy,' she says. 'I'll call you if I need you. Well, Mr Lea, let's get down to first name terms and then you can tell me all about it. I'm Cynthia Grimdyke.'

'Doctor Grimdyke?' I say. 'I wasn't expecting a woman. Not, of course, that it makes any difference. I'm Timothy Lea.'

'Sit down, Timothy.' I sit on one of those canvas chairs that suddenly tilts backwards and swallows your bum, and struggle into an upright position. 'That's right. Now, fire away. Don't hold anything back.'

'Well,' I say. 'It's very simple. I find that I'm no longer able to make love lying down. It's especially difficult if there is water about.'

'You mean, if it's raining?' says Doctor Cynthia.

'No,' I say. 'It's more the presence of water. Baths and taps and things like that.'

It seems so stupid when I say it, but Cynthia looks really interested. 'Fascinating,' she says. 'Quite, quite, fascinating.

I've never come across anyone like you before.' There is a long pause while she stares at me and I try and think of something to say. 'You did say taps, didn't you?'

'That's right,' I say.

'Have you ever thought about the shape of a tap?'

'Not especially,' I say.

'Don't they remind you of something?'

'Well-er –'

'A detumescent penis, for example?'

'Sorry-I-er-I –'

'Your penis is a bent tap. We've got to straighten it out. The water is immaterial.'

She sits back triumphantly and I try to figure out what she is talking about. 'I don't quite get it,' I say. 'I've never thought about taps like that.'

'Exactly' Doctor Cynthia snaps her fingers. 'That's the trouble. You've set up a blockage. By not facing up to the truth about your tap fixation you've created a whole lot of problems for yourself. You came to see me just in time. I may be able to save you.'

'That's marvellous,' I say. I mean it, too. If the doctor lady can straighten out my bent tap I will completely revise my opinion of the NHS.

'What do you do for a living?' asks Cynthia, swinging her legs sideways so that her thigh muscles curve temptingly.

'Plumbing, mainly,' I say. 'I'm a sort of glorified plumber's mate without a governor.'

Doctor Cynthia slaps one of the aforementioned thighs enthusiastically. 'Perfect!' she says. 'Don't you see? It all fits. You're like a man with hay fever working in a florists. Every time you see a tap it undermines the erectile potential of your penis.'

'Puts a kinkle in my winkle, you mean?' I say.

'Ye-es,' says the nice lady doctor. 'You could describe it

like that. Do you often play around with the vernacular?'

'Not since I was a kid,' I say. 'Dad used to say that it would stunt my growth.'

Doctor Cynthia looks puzzled for a moment and then nods her head sympathetically. 'I think I've got to the root of your problem. Taps rarely function except when they are set at right angles to the vertical. You regard your penis as being a tap and so you can not adjust yourself to sexual intercourse unless you are standing up. Eg vertical.'

'What about the water?' I say.

'Forget about the water.'

'But I can't forget about the water. Every time I lie down – whhooosh!!'

'Bed wetting?'

'No! The feeling that I'm going to be swept away by a great flood. Nausea. Dizziness.'

Doctor Cynthia remains silent for a few moments and I can sense her highly trained medical mind flicking through a lifetime of case histories. Finally, she speaks. 'I think the answer is that we mustn't rush things. We've slowly got to wean you from the vertical to the horizontal. We'll tackle the water business as it arises. I'm certainly not going to wash my hands in it – I mean, of it.'

'Thank you very much,' I say. 'What exactly did you have in mind?'

Doctor Cynthia takes a deep breath and looks purposeful. 'Have you heard of surrogates?' she asks.

'Oh yes,' I say. 'Very bracing. It's in Yorkshire, isn't it?'

'That's Harrogate,' says Cynthia through tight lips. 'Basically, a surrogate is a substitute.'

'Like in football,' I say brightly.

'Not quite like in football,' says Superdoc. I can see that her smile is beginning to fray round the edges. 'If you listen, I'll tell you all about it.'

'I'm all ears,' I say.

Doctor Cynthia Grimdyke folds her arms across her shapely knockers in businesslike fashion and begins to give me the gen. 'A disturbingly large number of couples in this country fail to achieve full sexual satisfaction. The causes are many and diffuse. I believe that the advice available today does not go far enough in getting down to the root of the problem. Textbook answers just aren't good enough. The only real guidance comes from practical involvement in the patient's problems.' I nod brightly like I know what she is talking about. 'If we can provide a surrogate, or substitute partner, to help you clear your sexual blockages then we will be well on the way to straightening you out.'

'You can get all that on the National Health?!' I say. 'Blimey! If I'd known that I'd have-er-um been much comforted in times of need.'

'It's an independent venture,' says Doctor Cyn. 'A matter purely between Judy and myself.'

'Judy?' I say.

'That's right. Our receptionist. The girl who showed you in here. She's very interested in this kind of thing. She won't mind me telling you that she had an unhappy marriage which she believes broke down because of unresolved sexual difficulties. She wants to put back into relationships what she herself failed to get out of them.'

'That's very admirable,' I say. 'You-er don't get-er involved, then?'

Doctor Cynthia shakes her finely sculptured nut from side to side. 'Only in very special cases. We have some patients who have to be weaned away from group sexual activity.'

'Funny you should say that,' I tell her. 'My trouble is worst when –'

Doctor Cyn dries me up with another shake of her head.

'No. I think it is best that I control this treatment from a position once removed. You will involve yourself with Judy, she will report back to me, and I will advise her on the procedures to be followed.'

'Right,' I say. 'I'll place myself completely in your hands – or rather, in Judy's hands – or rather –'

'Say no more. If you go through that door, I will brief Miss Gould and she will join you shortly. Take off your clothes and relax. You'll find some magazines in there.'

'You haven't got the March 1956 edition of *Scottish Field*, have you?' I ask. 'There was this article I was reading. I'd just got to the part where the doe was going to drop her calf. It's amazing how they do it, isn't it? I mean, it must be so parky in those glens –'

'We don't have any magazines like that,' husks Doctor Grimdyke. 'Our wild life is of a rather different nature.'

She flares out her nostrils and opens a door in the wall – one of the best places for them, incidentally. I pass through and cop an eyeful of a plainly furnished room dominated by a low double bed and a high-backed armchair. The bed does not have any pillows or blankets on it, just a few casually draped sheets. Behind the armchair is an open window with a drawn venetian blind trembling in the slight breeze. The room is therefore far less brightly lit than Doctor Grimdyke's surgery. More intimate, in fact.

'Make yourself at home. There's a bathroom through that door. The magazines are on the table.'

The door closes behind me and I am left on my tod. It is a pity that Doctor Grimdyke is not going to participate in my treatment. I quite fancied her. Still, you can't have everybody. I go over to the bathroom and take a gander at the magazines. Phew! I can see what Cynthia was getting at. They are like the stuff Dad used to hide in the hall stand – 'hall stand all-stand' I used to call it. You never saw so many erect hamptons – at least, I imagine you didn't. I have no idea what you get up to in your spare time.

I decide to return to the goodies later and go into the bathroom. There is a shower there so I strip off and turn myself into a lovely pink Timothy Lea with a few brisk rubs of the bath towel. There is also a blue towelling dressing-gown, presumably left behind by a midget as I discover when I slip it on.

Back to the main room and I pick up *The Spanker's Handbook*. It has an introduction by a military geezer whose face is vaguely familiar – no, not Field Marshal Montgomery – and a lot of interesting close-up shots. I don't fancy the wallpaper much and I wouldn't be seen dead in those socks – let alone doing what that bloke is doing – but I don't suppose that everybody is as sensitive as I am. Anyway, it succeeds in being hornier than a reindeer round-up and I am glad that I have the scant protection offered by the dressing-gown. Percy is rearing up as if he wants to look at the pictures for himself.

I have just started on 'Big day at the Lollypop Factory' – no sign of a lollypop, so far – when a soft click alerts me to the fact that the door to the corridor has been opened. As I adjust my dressing-gown, Judy comes in carrying a trestle and a plank.

'Sorry to be so long,' she says cheerfully. 'I had a bit of trouble finding the right equipment. I think this should do the trick.'

'What trick did you have in mind?' I say, trying to see if she is concealing a saw behind her back.

Judy laughs lightly and goes over to the window. 'This seems a good place, doesn't it?' she says, putting down the trestle and resting the plank against it in an upright position.

'I had to borrow this lot from the builders next door. You've no idea of the problems I had.'

When she bends over, I get an inkling of what she is talking about. She is still wearing the white coat, but not a lot else. I bet that cheered them up a bit. It is not having a bad effect on Lea and friend, either. I move towards the window with something approaching rapidity.

'Do you want to keep the magazine?'

'What? Oh-yes-I mean, no.' I chuck the magazine back on the pile.

'You can hang on to it if you want to.' I look down at the front of my dressing-gown. 'I meant the magazine. A lot of our patients find them very stimulating. The Japs use them a great deal.'

'You get a lot of Japs here, do you?' I ask, thinking that they always look as if they are wearing National Health dentures.

'No. I meant that they use them in Japan. Now –' Judy adapts a creditable imitation of Doctor Grimdyke's business-like manner '–let's get down to it – or rather, up to it – shall we?'

'I'm still not quite certain what I've got to do,' I say.

'It's terribly simple,' says Judy. 'Doctor Grimdyke thought of it. She's awfully clever. What we're going to do is have intercourse against this board when it's in the vertical position and then slowly tilt it backwards until, without you really being aware of it, you'll find that you're performing quite normally in the horizontal. The secret is going to be in the way we move the board. Bit by bit.'

'Sounds all right,' I say. In fact, it sounds blooming marvellous but I don't want to let on in case I appear like the crude, cock-happy custard I really am.

'You are acclimatised to the vertical position?'

'I think so,' I say trying to cast my mind back. 'I haven't

experienced any twinges that I can recall. Since I've had this dizziness problem it has cast a cloud over all aspects of my sex life.'

'Well, we'll see what we can do,' says Judy sympathetically. 'I'll lean against the board and you come here.'

Trying not to break into a run, I position myself as close to the lady as percy will allow. If I am to get any nearer she will have to throw open her state apartment to the pubic. Her shoulders are pressed firmly against the upright board and her white coat falls open to reveal the graceful curve of a breast.

'Do you feel all right?' she says. 'Yes, I can see that you do. Nothing shy about you, is there?'

'I try to conquer my natural timidity,' I say. 'That's what they used to call me, you know: "Timidity" Lea.'

'Really? That is funny.'

Despite her words, Judy seems more interested in getting to grips with my hampton. Her right hand slips inside my dressing-gown and closes greedily round my sex shooter. I brush my lips against her neck and send down a couple of digits to check out the natural resources. Just a touch tells me that the fruit is ripe for the plucking.

'Kiss me!'

I am glad she said that. I didn't know whether you necked on the National Health. It would be a bit clinical, otherwise, wouldn't it? Our minds must be working on the same lines because, just as I bend my knees, she stands on tiptoe. The result is that I am giving her grumble a rumble before you can say 'three times a day after meals'.

'Do you feel any ill effects?' I keep percy on the move and consider the question. On the whole – or rather, in the hole – I feel fine.

'Nothing at all,' I say. 'How about you?'

Judy smiles sweetly. 'It's lovely, but I'm not the one with

the problem. It's your feelings that matter.'

'But my feelings depend on your feelings. I'm not going to enjoy it as much in any position if you're getting nothing out of it.'

'That's very sweet of you.' Judy squeezes my biceps. 'Are you ready to tilt the board a bit?'

'I think so.'

'I think we can do it without – yes, that's it.' Without us having to separate, Judy taps back with her shoulders and the plank scrapes forward a few inches. I press my body firmly against my luscious surrogate and feel no ill effects. 'Still all right?'

'Smashing!' I say. 'I could do this all day.'

'I don't think that will be necessary. If we go on making progress – who knows?'

'Who knows, indeed?' I say. I bang away enthusiastically and the board tilts back another few inches.

'Careful,' says Judy. 'I felt it going then.'

'You must have been mistaken,' I say. 'I'm being very careful.'

'I meant the board,' pants Judy. 'It's a bit unsteady against the trestle – OOOOOh! That's just what the doctor ordered!'

'Do you need any help?' I turn my head to see that Doctor Grimdyke has appeared beside us. She is biting her lower lip and there is an expression of rapt attention on her face. It is difficult to concentrate with her hand doing that to my backside but I try and pull myself together.

'We want to move the board a bit,' I say.

'I'll try and help,' says Doctor C. 'If I rest my foot against it – how's that?'

'Not out,' I say with a light laugh.

'Great!' breathes Judy.

'Everything proceeding satisfactorily? No dizzy spells?'

'No problems,' I say, continuing to deal out stiff punishment with my giggle stick. 'Still, we haven't started to bend over backwards very far yet, have we?'

'A pleasure to come,' says the white hope of the NHS, plucking at the top of her Parker 51.

'It certainly is,' agrees Judy enthusiastically. 'OOOOOO-OHH!!'

Doctor Cyn begins to look harassed. 'I think we may have to relieve this surrogate,' she says through clenched teeth. 'I will take personal control of this session.'

I don't think Judy has heard because her mouth has dropped open and her eyes are closed as if she is experiencing physical pain. 'Judy!' says Cynthia sharply. 'Miss Gould!! Pull yourself together!'

I try and slacken my pelvic thrust but Judy pulls me closer to her and it is clear that she is going into orbit. 'I'm sorry,' I pant. 'I think you'll have to hang on a minute – *don't take your foot away from the board!!*'

But Doctor Grimdyke does take her foot away from the board. My last memory of her is standing back and impatiently ripping open the front of her white coat. The second that the restraining pressure of her foot is withdrawn, the plank flips over the low trestle and I find myself sliding over Judy and towards the window. Before I have completely woken up to what is happening my bonce has collided with the venetian blinds and then passed through them. I have a terrifying vision of a busy street spread out below me, and then I am flying through the air to meet it! The plank has become a chute that has fed me out of the window.

I steel myself for the concrete kiss of the pavement but what I hit turns out to be more like a striped trampoline. I bounce in the air, turn a somersault, and land on the awning of what turns out to be a greengrocers. I find this out when the awning splits and I drop six feet onto a display of peaches. A big bloke with a crinkly face and a bashed in hooter looks down at me in amazement.

' 'Ere!' he says. 'Whatya think you're doing?!'

A lot of women are screaming and running all over the place and I suppose you can't blame them. The remains of the venetian blind does not do a lot to hide my predicament – apart from anything else. I feel amongst the squashed peaches between my legs and produce a card which says. 'Please don't squeeze the merchandise when making your selection.' Very funny. I manage to raise myself on one elbow, and flash walnut features a brave smile.

'These peaches are a bit soft, aren't they, Henry?' I say.

CHAPTER EIGHT

In which Felicity and Nancy work their therapeutic magic at the Indoor Outdoor Exhibition and something very climactic happens.

'Right,' says Sid. 'Cock this one up and we're all in the brace and bit.'

'Yes, Sid,' I say.

'What's the matter with you?' says Sid. 'Perk yourself up for God's sake. You're like a piece of old chewing-gum before rigor mortis sets in.'

I have not told Sid about my problem. Going to him for sympathy would be like dunking your privates in a vat of sulphuric acid. Since my fortunate escape from the death of a thousand peach stones my sex life has not been anything to make editors of Sunday Newspapers outbid each other for my life story. My love dive from a second story window has – hardly surprisingly – done nothing to improve my attitude towards horizontal sex. In fact, I am not all that enthusiastic about performing vertically or even diagonally. I think that the best idea is to write me off as a sex object. The whole thing is vastly overrated. You are much better off with a pile of osiers and a good pattern book.

'Can you see Crispin?' says Sid. 'Look enthusiastic when he shows up for God's sake. He knows you're an idiot but show him that you're an enthusiastic idiot.'

Sid and Crispin – or Crispin, I don't know which – has got us this job as maintenance men at the Indoor Outdoor

Exhibition. We have to make sure that everything is 'ticking over' to use Crispin's phrase.

'There's enough stuff here, isn't there?' says Sid. 'Look at all those caravans.'

'I never fancied a caravan holiday,' I say.

'Who's talking about holidays?' says Sid. 'We're all going to be living in those soon. You won't be able to afford anything else. Stash one down the end of the garden and let your house to the Arabs while they decide what to do with the country. It's your best chance of making a few bob – either that or melting down Eric Morley's hair for the oil.'

'It's the boats that fascinate me,' I say. 'Especially that electrically controlled job that runs on land or water. You must have a fantastic mind to design a thing like that.'

'I didn't design it,' says Sid, modestly.

'I know you didn't!' I snap. 'I meant "you" in the widest sense. You couldn't design a hole in the side of a dough-nut.'

Sid takes umbrage at this remark but I pay no attention to him. Swinging towards me wearing trendy matelot gear and a superior expression is Imogen Fletcher. Her eyes drift across my face without showing any signs of recognition but I am not the kind of geezer to let a little thing like that phase me.

'Hi!' I say, extending my right hand and revolving it like I am wiping an invisible window pane. 'It's me!'

'Hello me,' says Imogen. She peers at me closely and her expression lightens. 'Oh yes,' she says. 'You're right. It is you. I didn't recognise you without your glasses.'

'I don't wear glasses,' I say.

'Well you should do, darling. You know it's bad for my eyes.' Mrs Fletcher gives a light laugh and I sense that she is in frisky mood. I wish I could say the same for something else not a million miles away from the slit in my Y-fronts. There was a time when the presence of the fair Imogen in the same building would have been enough to get me drawing bleeding hearts on the walls of the karsi. Now it is all I can do to scrawl 'Right' in front of 'Up The Gunners!'

'How are your ceramics?' continues Mrs Fletcher.

For a moment I wonder if she is a mind reader. Then it occurs to me that she must have got me mixed up with somebody else. 'I haven't got any,' I say.

'Oh, of course.' Mrs F snaps her fingers in annoyance. 'You're not Shade Balfour, are you?'

Before I can answer, Sid greases in at full crawl. 'Good morning, Imogen,' he purrs. 'Looking for a boat, are we?'

'Funnily enough, I am,' says Mrs F loftily. 'I think it would be rather fun for getting away from it all. The beaches are crowded with such ghastly people aren't they? At the first wisp of candy floss it could be up anchor and away.' She looks at Sid and me like we are the first people she would be trying to get away from. I reckon that Crispin must have been making a few disturbing reports about our working relationship. Wives are always the first ones to take umbrage.

Sid is so thick that he does not sense the coolness underlining Imogen's manner. 'Oh yes,' he says all posh-like. 'You can have a slap-up time slopping around on a sloop, can't you? Rosie's having a look at the moment. You might well bump into her. She's with my in-laws.'

I am quick to notice the expression of mingled fear and horror that flashes across Imogen's face at the mention of Mum and Dad. Obviously, memories of Sid's dinner party have been slow to die. 'I'll keep my eyes open for them,' says Imogen sounding as if she means it. 'Well, I'd better be moving on. There's so much to see.'

She drifts off and Sid and I continue to gaze at the marina.

Yes, they have built this enormous indoor lake with boats moored all round it. It looks just like a real life harbour as I imagine it. There is even a painted back drop made to look like Prospero or some other Cornish fishing village.

'It's a lovely craft, that SK 498, isn't it?' says Sid. 'A miracle of British craftsmenship. Fifty knots in water and a hundred and twenty on the M1 when the cops aren't watching. It just shows that when we set our minds to it, we can beat the world.'

'It's the radar that gets me,' I say. 'How you can put it on to automatic so that it veers away from any other vessel that strays into its path. What a boon in congested waterways or when it's foggy.'

'Exactly,' says Sid. 'And the birds are a bit of all right, aren't they?'

Normally, the birds would have been the first things I would have commented on. There are two of them, one blonde, one redhead. The SK498 cruises round the marina and they lie on the roof of the cabin structure wearing bikinis and big smiles. The knockers on them make you think of four steam puddings lying in a hammock.

'Look,' says Sid. 'They're waving to us. I wonder what they want?'

'They're just waving, Sid,' I say dispiritedly. 'That's what they're paid to do.'

'I don't know what's come over you,' says Sid. 'Where's your Viking spirit? This is the land of Frobisher, Drake, Raleigh and Richard Todd, you know.'

'It's also Earls Court on a wet Monday,' I say. 'The gutters still full of sleeping Australians, the –'

'All right, all right,' says Sid. 'That's enough of that. Look! They're coming over.'

Sid is right. The SK 498 with the blonde bird at the tiller is steering straight for us. 'Ahoy there, landlubbers,' sings out the redheaded bint. 'Are you paying maintenance or giving it?'

The witty creature is clearly referring to the word '*Maintenance*' emblazoned across Sid's and my chest.

'I don't think we'd be able to do much with that,' says Sid with praiseworthy caution. 'You'd better get on to the designer, hadn't you?'

'No need to bother him,' says the blonde bint. 'It's terribly trivial. Anyway, he's at the Ritz with a trade delegation. We haven't seen him for three days. Come on! Be a couple of sports. A quick trip round the bay won't do you any harm.'

I look at Sid questioningly but he has already flung his leg over the bulwark – it's all right, he suffers no permanent damage. We have just clambered into the cockpit when Crispin Fletcher hoves into view. Immediately he sees us, a worried expression invades his face.

'Not gallivanting, I hope?' he says sternly. 'You remember what I said, Sidney!'

'Definitely,' says Sid, practically touching his forelock in his desire to please. 'Absolutely. Oh yes. We're just going to sort out these two young ladies.'

It would not be so bad if the two birds did not start giggling. 'What?!' says Fletcher, anxiety mingling with menace. I have never seen him so dominant before. I suppose that working with Sid makes anyone feel dominant.

'What's the problem?' hisses Sid to one of the birds.

'We can't make the bottle opener work,' says the redhead.

'We're going to fix the bot-bot-bottom of the boat.' The last four words come out in an ugly rush as Sid struggles to find an alternative to the less than reassuring truth. Fletcher is still looking unhappy as we skim out to the middle of the marina.

'Why didn't you say "Aye, aye, skipper" or something?'

says Sid. 'Remember how important this is to us. Without Crispin we'd be finished. It wouldn't be worth carrying on.'

'I'm not a crawler, like you,' I say contemptuously. 'I'm not prepared to grovel to anyone – oh, let me take that.' I swiftly remove the tray of glasses that the blonde is carrying out of the cabin.

'Better not have drinkies on desk, Felicity,' says the redhead. 'Some old fuddy duddy will complain.'

'Righto, Nancy,' says the blonde. 'Into the jolly old cabin we go. You chaps will join us for a spot of grog, won't you?'

'A drink?' says Sid cautiously. 'Well, that would be very nice. Just a small one while we're on the job.' The two birds look at each other and I wonder what has come over Sid. He is always a bit inclined to be like me – uneasy in the presence of posh tarts, and Nancy and Felicity are clearly very establishment. Personally, if a bird has big tits, I find it easy to think of her as being common like me. Large knockers and refinement never go hand in hand as far as I am concerned.

Nancy carries the tray back into the cabin and we follow her. All the time, the boat is weaving round the pool under its own steam. If it comes near anything else, it veers off at an angle. It is amazing really.

'Where's this-er bottle opener?' says Sid.

'Right here on the bulkhead,' says Nancy.

'The wall,' says Felicity, helpfully.

'Oh yes,' says Sid, stepping away from a ventilation grill. 'I was looking for something bigger. Now, what's the trouble? It looks straightforward enough to me. You just put the bottle in the slot, twist, and – hey presto!'

'Oh!' says Felicity, brushing her tawny hair from her lightly freckled cheek. 'It's easy, isn't it? We hadn't been doing it like that.'

'It's all a question of how you put it in,' says Sid. Once

again, the birds look at each other and start giggling. 'You are awful!' says Nancy.

'Are you trying to get us arrested?' I hiss.

'Shut up!' says Sid, blushing scarlet.

'I'm afraid there's only Southern Courage,' says Felicity holding up what looks like a whisky bottle. 'It's the drink of the Deep South.'

'You mean Penge?' says Sid.

'The deep south of America!' I inform him. Honestly, Sid is about as sophisticated as a farting contest. I pick up the bottle and read the label: 'Southern Courage is a mellow blend of eleven different spirits, one for each state in the Confederacy. The drink that lost the South the American Civil War'.

'Do you remember the Yank who left that?' says Nancy, rolling her eyes.

'Could I ever forget?' says Felicity.

'Sounds potent,' says Sid.

'Oh, he was!' Both girls shriek with laughter and take playful swipes at Sid who covers his face with his hands.

'I was talking about the drink!' he whines.

'Look,' I say, glad to be able to change the subject. 'There are Mum and Dad and Rosie.'

'And the Fletchers,' says Sid. 'Oh, I hope your Dad doesn't say anything out of place.'

'You can talk!' I say.

'Don't wave!' says Sid. 'We don't want them to see us with –' he lowers his voice '– these birds. You know what Rosie's like. She's broken the world record for jumping to conclusions.'

'It's too late,' I say. 'They've already seen us – hey! Watch it, Mum! Did you see that? She nearly fell in.'

The Leas and Fletchers are exchanging a few words that neither of them need on the foredeck of a smart white yacht moored by the side of the marina. A geezer in yachting cap and blazer is hovering hopefully with an order book. I notice that as Mum nearly falls in, Dad is swift to grab Imogen Fletcher by the knockers. Another tremor and he will probably give her artificial respiration.

'Does your Dad swim?' says Sid wistfully. 'I wish I had a few man-eating sharks handy.'

'Down the hatch, chaps. Thanks most awfully for the assistance.' Felicity shoves a couple of tumblers into our mits and I notice that the Southern Courage bottle is now half empty. 'It must be wonderful to be mechanically minded.'

'It's just a knacker,' says Sid. 'I mean, a knack!'

'He's incorrigible, isn't he?' says Nancy. 'What are we going to do with him?' She turns to me. 'Are you naughty, too?'

A few minutes before I would have had no trouble answering her, but now I am not so sure. That Southern Courage stuff is a lot stronger than diluted Tizer – not much different in taste but a lot stronger. My head seems to be going round in the opposite direction to the boat. 'I'm pretty naughty,' I say. 'You're pretty in any condition.' Notice how the old verbal magic has come back in a flash. I haven't felt like saying anything nice to a bird for days.

'Thank you,' says Nancy. 'That is nice. How refreshing to find that the spirit of romance is not dead.'

'I reckon that this stuff must be the spirit of romance,' says Sid, nodding at his glass. 'I feel fruitier than a two-ton banana.'

'Funny you should say that,' I say. 'I feel quite frisky myself.'

'It's rude to whisper,' says Felicity. 'Let's all share it.'

'What a good idea!' says Sid, knocking back the rest of

his drink. 'Come here, darling and I'll show you an old knee shanty I learned when I was in the Sea Scouts.'

'A sea shanty, not a knee shanty,' I say.

'Listen, mate,' says Sid, an ugly note creeping into his voice. 'You stick to your sea shantys and I'll stick to my knee shantys!'

'And I'll be in Scotland afore ye!' trills Felicity. 'I say, how ripping it all is!' With these words, she bounds into Sid's arms and her bikini top hits the floor seconds later. It could not happen at a worst moment because I see Rosie peering through a porthole as we sweep past the yacht. I only catch a glimpse of her but the expression on her mug suggests that she has copped a full gander at her old man fluffing up Felicity's tititties. There is a bunk on either side of the cabin and Sid and his chick flop on to one of them like we are playing 'Feet Off Ground'.

I turn to see how Nancy is taking all this and find her topless and practically bottomless. 'Worse things happen at sea,' she breathes, stepping out of her bikini panties.

'I don't know if it's the boat or the booze,' I say. 'But I feel all –' I stumble back against the empty bunk and Nancy drops to her knees and starts pulling my shoes off.

'I know,' she murmurs. 'I felt like that before we finished the first bottle.'

'How many have you – ?'

'Three,' she says, biting the inside of my thigh through my jeans. 'Come on, I'm crazy for it!'

A desire so delicately expressed is calculated to win a response from a heart of stone and in less time than it takes to roll a new rubber down the handle of your cricket bat, I am nuder than a peeled grape. Nancy is pegged out beneath me and the narrow bunk makes a prison for our heaving flanks.

'Kiss me! Harder!' shouts my impressionable friend and I suddenly realise what Nelson's last words must have been. I suddenly realise something else, as well. The boat seems to be going very fast. I glance out of a port hole and see a blurr of movement as we flash past one of the yachts. It is bobbing up and down at its mooring like a cork.

'Sid –!' I cry – but there is no Sid. I glance back and see that the stupid berk is fondling Felicity at the top of the companionway – amongst other places. Everybody must be able to see them. 'Sid!' I scream. 'What are you doing?! Let go of those controls!'

Sid must have blundered against some mechanism that programmes the speed of the boat because we are going round the marina at about eighty miles an hour. The wash from our wake is breaking over some of the smaller boats and – oh my gawd! That is Mum hanging over the side of that yacht. And what is Dad doing to that woman he has just pulled from the water?! Thank goodness the boat suddenly changes direction and all I can see is Crispin Fletcher and Rosie diving below the surface to get out of our way. 'Stop screaming with maniacal laughter and do something, Sid!' I shout. 'No! Not that!!'

You would not think it was possible at the speed we are going. And standing up, too.

'Stop flapping, darling!' chides the chick beneath my thighs. 'It's only a bit of fun. Whheeeeeeeeeeeee!!!!' She clamps her hands over my back bumpers like Tower Bridge coming down fast and rocks me backwards and forwards against her body.

'Pull another lever, Sid!' I shout. 'You've got to slow us down!'

'Up the workers!' yells Sid. He takes a last swig from the Southern Courage bottle and throws it over his shoulder. There is a scream of pain from a male voice. It may be my imagination but it sounds suspiciously like Crispin Fletcher.

'You have to put it on manual if you want to control it,' pants Nancy. 'Come on, darling. Our rhythm is faltering.'

'Put it on manual!' I shout. I would do it myself but you have less chance of getting away from Nancy than you do of cancelling a subscription to *The Reader's Digest*. Not that I am all that keen to get away from Nancy. She is a very beautiful girl and it is a long time since – suddenly. I wake up to what I am doing. I am actually having it off with a bird and suffering no ill effects. And I am doing it horizontally and on – 'Sid!' I shout. 'Sid, I –'

'All right, all right! Belt up, will you?!' Sid reaches behind Felicity and presses something. Felicity screams so he presses something else. Immediately, the boat surges towards the back drop of the Cornish fishing harbour.

'I'm cured! I'm cured!' I blather. 'Oh Nancy! You don't know what this means to me.'

'It is lovely,' agrees my new friend obviously not understanding the true nature of my ecstasy. 'Go on! I'm coming.'

There is an enormous thump – for which I am only partly responsible – and the boat runs smoothly again.

'It's wonderful, Sid!' I shout. 'Wonderful. And what's more, I'm doing it on water.'

'Not any more, you're not!' I raise my head and look back to see what looks like an enormous sheet of paper with a hole in the middle of it. It is disappearing fast. 'What the –' BANG!! Two enormous iron exit doors crash open and we roar out into the street.

'Oh!' says Felicity sounding really worried. 'We weren't supposed to demonstrate it on the road until the Motor Show.'

Sid dives for the steering wheel and we pass a double decker bus on the inside travelling at about eighty. It is unfortunate that the bus is travelling in the opposite direction to us.

'If we want to be home for tea,' I say. 'You'd better head for Battersea Bridge. The traffic builds up something terrible at this time of the day.'

'Groovy!' says Nancy. 'I think there's another bottle of Southern Courage in that locker.'

CONFESSIONS OF A NIGHT NURSE

Rosie Dixon

IT WASN'T SO MUCH A QUESTION OF LOSING HER VIRGINITY AS OF MISLAYING IT.

Rosie Dixon really did want to save herself for Mr. Right but things had a habit of getting on top of her. Like that party which got out of hand and made her parents so angry they asked her to leave home.

Not to worry. Queen Adelaide's Hospital always had room for a warmhearted girl with a willing pair of hands.

At a big hospital like that she couldn't help bumping into men. Rosie soon made a name for herself as every patient's dream, matron's nightmare and doctor's dilemma.

CONFESSIONS FROM THE POP SCENE

Timothy Lea

Teenyboppers, hungry groupies, payola, crooked DJs, foreign tours, golden discs, TV spectaculars, screaming fans and packed out concert halls . . .

For Timmy Lea, always on the lookout for a new career with plenty of openings, Noggo Enterprises spelled success, money and a chance to get his name into the bright lights — providing he could survive the partnership with brother-in-law Sid and his nephew Jason Nuggett, the 7-year-old's answer to Mick Jagger, not to speak of Dyke Henna, the transvestite rock star (born Fred Nudger).

Even when business was slow, the manager of Noggo Enterprises found plenty of scope for his talents; in beds, bars and the back seats of sportscars there was always somebody who wanted a little piece of his action.

Would simple, unaffected Timmy survive in the hard world of Pop?